HUM

HUM

STORIES

MICHELLE RICHMOND

FC2

TUSCALOOSA

Copyright © 2014 by Michelle Richmond

The University of Alabama Press

Tuscaloosa, Alabama 35487-0380

All rights reserved

Manufactured in the United States of America

FC2 is an imprint of The University of Alabama Press

Book Design: Illinois State University's English Department's
 Publications Unit; Codirectors: Steve Halle and Jane L.
 Carman; Assistant Director: Danielle Duvick; Production Assistant: Eric Austin
 Longfellow

Cover Design: Lou Robinson

Typeface: Garamond

⊗

The paper on which this book is printed meets the minimum requirements of American National Standard for Information Sciences—Permanence of Paper for Printed Library Materials, ANSI Z39.48–1984

Library of Congress Cataloging-in-Publication Data

Richmond, Michelle, 1970-

   [Short stories. Selections]

Hum : Stories / Michelle Richmond.

      pages cm

   ISBN 978-1-57366-178-2 (paperback : alk. paper) — ISBN 978-1-57366-845-3 (ebook)

   I. Title.

   PS3618.I35A6 2014

   813'.6—dc23

                                  2013039256

FOR KEVIN

CONTENTS

FOREWORD

BY RIKKI DUCORNET

Told with intelligence and lucidity, "Hum" opens this collection; the story's momentum, too, is impressive. *Hum* is disquieting and masterful, emblematic of a book given over to the study of couplings coming undone. Like the synthetic smells of gunpowder, sex and blood incessantly pumped into the movie theater across the street, the hum that overtakes and undermines a marriage indicates the dilemma that eats at the heart of lives unsettling, surprising and always arresting. Here the central theme is risk and the paramount inquiry is need— the need to be unshackled, tested and amazed; the imperious need for heat, for transformation ("Change is near!"), for anything perceptibly flammable, for "the desperate sweetness of hotel rooms."

In "Scales" an irresistible stranger covered with horny scales reaches into a paper bag and hands a boiled crayfish to the young woman he has just met and who will become his lover. Fascinated by his strangeness and longing "to embark on something terrible and fine" she breaks off the head and sucks the juices greedily. Clearly the affair is made in heaven (as they say); its hellish aspects are manageable, even thrilling (his scaled body is highly abrasive)—but it is his transformation into something like normalcy that proves unsupportable. (Most often the very things that bind these ill-fated couples are the very things that pull them apart.)

At their best these stories are wonderfully strange, a strangeness both compelling and convincing. In an unexpectedly deft and moving moment, a clinically acceptable hand job undertaken with surgical gloves becomes the surprising and deeply moving portal to the memory of a vanished sister.

The squelched and dissolving love affairs and marriages, not so much embattled as expended, unfold just a step away from a world that is dissolving, too. Yet the world is always tantalizing; after all, it is all there is. When the young wife in "Hum" says: "…I felt a quiet, guilty thrill as if I had been invited to play some mysterious and possibly dangerous game, the stakes of which were unclear," she is providing a key to the entire collection. Later she asks: "Does loneliness constitute an emergency?" These thoughtfully imagined stories convince us that it does.

HUM

HUM

We could hear it from any point in the house—upstairs, downstairs, even the garage. From the kitchen the sound was faint, like the upswing of a snore with no silent intervals in between, all intake of breath, no release. While we were eating at the small table by the window, forks and knives clicking against our plates, it was there in the background, a reminder. If we spoke loudly, the hum could be drowned out for a moment. In the beginning we tried, it was like a game, we attempted to keep a dialogue going during the entire dinner just to cover the hum with the sound of our voices. This went on for our first few weeks in the house, but there were only the two of us there, we knew each other well, and there was not much to be said. At one point, without ever voicing a mutual decision, we gave up. We fell into long silences, just the click of silverware on plates, the sound of wine being poured into a glass, the polite chewing—and beneath it all, or above it, the continual hum coming from the second bedroom, the source of our livelihood and of our growing discontent.

With music we could disguise it, could forget it for three or four minutes at a time, but there was always the moment when one song ended, the tinny whir of the CD player while it moved on to the next, so that, eventually, even music lost its joy for me.

At night, from our room across the hall, we could hear it. "It's just white noise," my husband said. "If you'd stop thinking about it, you wouldn't notice it at all." So I tried to stop thinking about it, but the more I tried, the louder it became. My unease was intensified by the fact that we were not allowed to go into the second bedroom; in fact, we had never even seen it.

Twice a month someone would stop by to check the equipment. He or she would arrive unannounced and knock discreetly on the side door. Often, this person would bring a cake or a bottle of wine, so that it would look to our neighbors as though a friend had come calling. Once inside, he would avoid conversation and head straight for the second bedroom, toting a large duffle bag. Never once did any of the maintenance personnel— that's how they always introduced themselves, not by name, but simply, "Hello, I'm the maintenance personnel"—agree to stay for coffee. Their abruptness heightened my sense that, even though we were merely caretakers of the equipment, not its subjects, we were under its scrutiny twenty-four hours a day.

Because the equipment had to be supervised round the clock, my husband and I never went anywhere together. If we wanted to see a movie, we would toss a coin. The winner would walk down the street, past the rows of primly painted mansions, the neat driveways with expensive cars, across the city road, to the Cinaromaplex. The place was so named because of the machines that piped appropriate smells into the theater during movies—the smell of gunpowder during a gunfight scene, smoke and liquor during a bar scene. The Cinaromaplex was even equipped with the musty scent of sex for certain R-rated movies, and for the more gruesome films, there was the distinct, metallic odor of blood. The winner of the coin toss would come home straight after the movie, and the one who had been house-sitting would go to the next showing. Later we would discuss the movie as if we had seen it together, as if we were an ordinary couple who went on outings as a pair, rather than as two halves.

It was the same way with restaurants, plays, and museums. When we first moved into the house, we made a pact that we would not sacrifice these small pleasures, the many cultural offerings of our beloved city. We decided to live as we always had, with minor adjustments. For a while we honored the pact, but about the same time we stopped insisting on dinner conversation we also ceased our elaborate efforts to see the same movies, eat at the same restaurants, view the same museum exhibits. The inevitable result was that, over time, we became more like roommates than a couple.

That is not to say I was entirely without companionship.

Some nights, unable to sleep, I would step into the backyard in my bathrobe. I would leave the porch light off, so as not to be seen, and would stand there in the dark, the wet grass slippery underfoot, and watch the Uradian Embassy. I would gaze up at the third floor corner window, where the light was always on, and I would watch the ambassador sitting at his desk, his tie pulled askew. I could never really make out his face, just the figure of him there. He sat as still as a man could possibly sit, and

I wondered what he was doing awake, night after night, while everyone else in the building slept.

I wanted to call up to him. I wanted to tell him about the second bedroom, and the machinery that hummed behind the closed door. I wanted to tell him about the dissolution of his country, a dissolution which, to him, might be only the vaguest fear, or perhaps even a nightmare he thought would likely come true—but no matter how vivid the nightmare, how disturbing his fears might have been, he could not have known for certain that his country was being slowly dissembled at that very moment, and that the machinery of its destruction hummed in the stately red brick house behind him. This is what the equipment did: it listened, it watched, it recorded everything.

Those nights, standing in my borrowed yard and staring up at the ambassador's window, I began to wonder if it is possible to love a man you have never met, if love can be born out of sympathy alone, and out of the knowledge that one's own life's work is intricately connected to the ruination of another. Could I love him simply for his insomnia, for the square of light cast by his window onto my sleeping lawn, for the knowledge that, without him, my own life would in some manner be rendered pointless?

I decided that I could.

I did not tell my husband about my late-night trips to the garden, although some nights he must have woken and found me gone. I did not tell him that I dreamed of this man's country, of miles and miles of unused train tracks ending in abandoned towns, of once-prosperous markets that were now home to a lonely clerk guarding a few loaves of bread, a single poor cut of meat. I did not tell him that there were days when I sat for hours imagining myself in the ambassador's country, starting a new life with him there.

Isn't it true that everyone, at some point, dreams of beginning anew—with new friends, new surroundings, a new lover? Doesn't everyone, at least once, dream of abandoning her own life?

***

My husband and I had become caretakers of the equipment by virtue of timing. The opportunity arose through a friend I had met years earlier while working as an administrative assistant in a government building. One afternoon in June, I ran into my old friend in a coffee shop. I mentioned that the landlord was raising our rent and we were going to have to move to a cheaper apartment across the river.

"Perhaps we can help each other," he said. "Do you have a few minutes?"

Over a cup of coffee, my friend explained that a trustworthy couple of impeccable discretion was needed immediately to inhabit a very nice home in the Duncan Hill District. "Should you be approved and choose to take on the task, you would be rewarded with free rent and household expenses."

Duncan Hill was a dream, the kind of tastefully wealthy neighborhood I would never have imagined myself living in. The homes there had the best river views in the city, and the boutiques that lined the neighborhood's main street sold one-of-a-kind dresses and handbags that cost more than I made in a month.

"What's the catch?"

"If you are selected, you'll have to be very careful," my friend said, biting into his almond biscotti. "You couldn't have visitors, the department would retain the right to enter the house at their discretion, and the second bedroom would be strictly off-limits. Most important, under no circumstances would you be allowed to have contact with anyone from the Uradian Embassy. Think of it as a luxurious house arrest."

I talked it over with my husband, he agreed, and after a quick but extensive background check and a series of intense interviews, we were approved. We moved in quietly on a Saturday, and that night we celebrated with champagne on the balcony overlooking our small, well-maintained backyard. "What do you suppose is going on in there?" my husband whispered, tipping his glass toward the embassy.

"That's exactly the kind of question you're not supposed to ask."

I glanced up at the embassy, and that was when I saw the ambassador for the first time, standing in a square of light in the third-floor corner window. He seemed to be staring out toward the river, but there was no moon that night, no way he could have seen the water in the darkness. Our own lights were off, so we must have been invisible to him. He reached up to loosen his tie, and I felt a quiet, guilty thrill, as if I had been invited to play some mysterious and possibly dangerous game, the stakes of which were unclear.

***

The ambassador's country, which was so small that the media rarely took notice of it, had managed several years before to get on the wrong side of my own government. Our government had attempted, first through economic and political pressures and later through a coup, to oust the prime minister, whose presence they considered to be a threat in the region. The coup had failed, in large part because it lacked the support of the citizenry, and ever since then a few dozen of our sharpest political and military minds had been working to slowly ruin Urada from the inside.

Over time, their efforts were proving successful. Urada's bank system was in a shambles, all four of its major industries had been brought to their knees, and violent splits had emerged within the major political parties. The most recent elections had erupted into riots so widespread that the elections had to be postponed indefinitely. The country appeared to be on the brink of civil war. A high-ranking official of our government took advantage of the riots to make a public statement that we were willing to "step in on behalf of the people" should the situation grow worse.

In the aftermath of the riots, I had seen the ambassador on television, firmly holding his ground. "Our leaders are aware," he said, "that 'step in' is merely a euphemism for foreign troops, martial law, and Urada's loss of sovereignty."

I did not know whether it was a trick of television cameras, or instead a trick of the third-floor window, but the ambassador appeared much larger on television than he did from my back-yard. He had dark hair giving way slightly to gray, blue eyes, a prominent forehead, and a faint scar traversing the bridge of his nose—all of which, taken together, made him attractive in an unsettling way. He always wore a light blue tie and dark suit, and on television he seemed to be in perpetual motion, his hands moving nervously as he spoke. If I could have talked to him in person, I would have told him that stillness suited him better, that those nights alone in his office he seemed possessed of a natural authority. But I could never speak to him. I could only admire him from afar.

***

Originally, moving into the house seemed like a wise decision. A year before, my husband and I had both given up stable office jobs to pursue more fulfilling careers. I had gone into fashion design, a lifelong dream, and my husband had become a personal trainer. Both of us failed to make enough money to survive. After our meager savings ran out, I took a position managing an exclusive boutique, and my husband gave up the idea of a private practice and went to work for a gym. Since most of our earnings went to pay the rent, we had abandoned our dream of buying a home in the city. This new arrangement would help us save money for a down payment on a house of our own.

I secretly relished the idea of working in tandem with my husband, with a shared goal and a shared secret; perhaps it would help to rekindle a lost camaraderie between us.

As it turned out, however, we rarely saw each other except on weekends and a couple of hours between shifts. I would come home from a day spent catering to wealthy socialites, exchange a few polite words with my husband before he left for work, and take a long, hot shower. I would step out of the shower and into the humming house, put on a bathrobe, and pad barefoot downstairs. I would make myself a small dinner and sit alone at the kitchen table, waiting for darkness to fall. Then I would wander out to the backyard and look up at the corner window. More often than not, the ambassador would be there within the square of light, a dark shape at his desk, sometimes writing or talking on the phone, but usually just sitting completely still. It struck me that he was a supremely lonely man, that we would make the perfect couple.

It was not our job to view the material being gathered in the second bedroom, or to relay information about the goings-on within the austere embassy building. We did have a key, but it was only to be used by direct order from the department or in case of extreme emergency.

I put this question to you now: Does loneliness constitute an emergency? What about despair? Add to this an unsettling attraction, perhaps affection, that slowly builds to something that, by some definitions, might be called love. Is this, then, an emergency? What would you have done faced with the figure in the window, the ongoing ache of wanting to know him, and the distance imposed by two governments locked in a philosophical war? And in a kitchen drawer, hidden beneath the napkins and coffee filters, beneath the plaid contact paper, a key. You have tried to forget it is there, but it is impossible. Night after night, as the hum vibrates through the house, you run your fingers over the small, solid shape of the key.

***

I began to do research. The ambassador was only 44 years old, younger than I had imagined. He grew up in a small industrial village in southern Urada, where he excelled in school. At the age of 16, he earned an art scholarship to the University of Urada, where he supplemented his studio courses in painting and drawing with difficult seminars in international law. Upon graduation he worked for several years as a law clerk before moving to England to take an advanced degree in business at Oxford. He did not complete his degree, but instead returned to Urada and ran for a minor office in the town where he grew up. From there, he worked his way up the political ladder.

A few weeks into my research, I discovered an interesting fact on an obscure blog written by an Uradian university student: the ambassador had been one of several hundred children orphaned by a factory disaster in the early sixties, and from the age of five until he left for college, he had been shuttled from relative to relative. There was a photograph of the ambassador at the age of seven, standing in the first row of a group of several dozen schoolchildren. The photograph suggested the usual boisterousness and chaos that attends large groups of children, but the young boy who would become the ambassador seemed frozen in place as he stared into the camera, arms crossed over his chest. I too was an orphan. I too had spent my childhood in many different houses, among many different adults. The orphan moves through life with a peculiar loneliness only another orphan can understand, always feeling not quite one with the world.

***

In November, five months after we moved into the house, there was a sudden flurry of activity. Instead of coming twice a month, the maintenance personnel began appearing at our door once a week. By the end of December it was three times a week. In early January, five hundred of our soldiers arrived in Urada on a "peacekeeping mission." The event hardly made the news—just ten seconds on CNN's World Minute, slightly better coverage on BBC. Only by searching the small stories far back in the newspaper did I discover that the ambassador had bluntly criticized the action. "This is clearly a military occupation disguised as something benign," he said.

There was no public outcry to speak of; even the most vociferous of the left remained silent. No one seemed to know where Urada was or what we were doing there.

During my nocturnal visits to the garden, I noticed that the ambassador was spending less and less time at his desk, more and more time staring out the window, yet he never so much as glanced my way. I had expended so much of my emotional energy on him, so much of my time, and he did not even know I existed. It reminded me of a terrible crush I had for three years in high school on a boy one grade above me, a boy I never met. When the object of my affection graduated, I felt a deep sense of regret for never having spoken to him, never having made myself known. I was a shy teenager with few friends, and after the boy disappeared from the school I felt an overwhelming sense of despair. Now, it was as if that high school crush was being repeated, albeit with much higher stakes.

One night in early February I went so far as to turn the light on in the garden and stand in a spot easily visible from the ambassador's window. I willed him to look at me. At one point, he did glance in my direction. I could not tell if it was merely a tick of his neck, or if he acknowledged me with a small nod.

In March, the number of troops in Urada increased to 1,000 and our government promised to send more, bandying about a number of noble words that rolled off their tongues with terrifying ease. "Freedom," our president said, "duty," uttering the words with such conviction one might surmise that God himself was leading the whole operation. The discussion of Urada took up fewer than three minutes of an hour-long press conference. Soon thereafter the ambassador called a press conference of his own, which was attended by only half a dozen reporters. "This has gone too far," he said. "All we ask is that you leave our country in peace."

***

Three months after the occupation began, I felt myself giving in. It was eight o'clock on a Thursday evening and my husband was working the late shift. I was alone in the house. I had taken my shower and enjoyed a simple dinner of salad and cold chicken. I was sitting in the study, well into my third glass of wine, listening to soft music. Each time a song came to a close, I felt my throat tightening, my whole body tensing, as I waited for the humming interval between songs.

The hum, that night, seemed louder than ever. What was it about the hum that bothered me so? It was annoying, certainly, but it was more than that. The hum reminded me of *him*, and when I thought of him I could not help but consider my own invisibility. The hum was a constant reminder that he did not see me. His country, too, was invisible, noticed only by a few powerful men who viewed it as a small, easily surmountable obstacle.

It was by some subconscious impulse that I found myself in the kitchen, staring into the open drawer, my fingers traveling over the contact paper. Only after I had peeled the paper from the wood, loosened the piece of tape that held the key, and slipped the key into my palm, did I realize what I was doing.

I walked down the hallway to the second bedroom. I hesitated only for a moment. Then, as if of its own will, the key slid into the doorknob. I expected something quite different, I suppose—alarms, bright lights, at the very least some resistance from the doorknob. But there was nothing, just the key sliding easily into place, clicking slightly as I turned it to the right, the doorknob yielding to my hand, the door swinging open.

I fumbled along the wall and found the light switch. The room was smaller than our bedroom, the walls adorned with a fussy floral wallpaper that must have been chosen decades before by the original owners. Inside the room, the hum was even louder, a steady, high-pitched whine. The room was filled with computers, unidentifiable gadgets, tiny TV screens. Each screen was labeled: green room, blue room, meeting hall, entryway, dining hall, bedroom 1, bedroom 2, and so forth.

It was not the meeting rooms and offices that interested me, the large tables around which important matters were discussed. Nor the sound of serious voices, discussing Urada's fate. What I desired was a more intimate picture—not of the ambassador, but of the man.

I walked from screen to screen until I found one labeled *Ambassador's Personal Suite*. I pulled a chair up to the television, took a moment to gather my nerves, and leaned in close. The screen was dark and grainy. I could make out a bed, a dresser, a rug. It took a few moments to focus, for my eyes to translate the moving shapes, but then it became clear—two bodies on the bed, the man partially clothed, the woman entirely naked.

Of course, what did I expect? He was doing what people do when their worlds fall apart: he was making love to his wife. There was no audio, just the movement of their bodies, and all around me, the high-pitched hum. I sat for several minutes, staring at the screen. The chair creaked each time I so much as shifted a knee, and I imagined an indistinct someone in some other dark room, listening in, noting the exact time the second bedroom was breached.

Eventually the ambassador stood up and wandered away from the bed, into what must have been the bathroom. The woman lay naked on her side. A couple of minutes later the ambassador returned. I watched them fall asleep. I could see the rise and fall of their chests as they breathed. At some point I realized that I was breathing with them, the three of us in tandem, a synchronized trio of breath. I put the chair in its original place, closed the door behind me, and returned the key to the kitchen drawer, pressing the contact paper down around it.

At four in the morning I heard the front door open, my husband's footsteps in the foyer. He came into the living room, and in his face I could see he was startled to find me awake, sitting in the chair by the fireplace.

He walked over and sat on the arm of the chair, touched my face.

"Why are you crying?" he asked.

"I don't know."

"Come to bed."

I allowed him to lead me there.

My husband was not an uncaring man. He was not without intellect or charm. As far as I knew, he had never been unfaithful. He was not to blame for the fact that, over time, we had become quietly lost to each other.

In April the number of troops rose again, this time to 2,500. I continued to make my nightly trips to the garden. One night, the ambassador did not appear in his window. Not the next night, or the next. Had he left the country? Had he relinquished his post? I searched the back pages of the paper for news of him, but there was nothing.

***

One afternoon in April, I left my husband to housesit while I went to see a movie at the Cinaromaplex. The title of the movie was *Countdown Emergency!* It was the kind of mindless blockbuster to which I have always been partial, the kind of movie that allows me to relax completely and forget my worries. When I arrived, however, it was already sold out. Rather than returning home to face my husband, who had been asking a lot of questions over the last few days—Why was I so quiet? Was I hiding something? Had he done something to upset me?—I bought a ticket to an independent film from Bulgaria that had received international acclaim, exactly the type of film I always tried to avoid. Subtitles, delicate characterizations of angst-ridden individuals, and political subtexts never failed to leave me depressed and anxious.

The poster for the Bulgarian film called it "enlightening and thought-provoking." I was not in the mood to be enlightened. I had come to the movies to clear my mind. The image I most wanted to erase was that of the ambassador's wife lying naked on the bed. Even with the blurry distance of the surveillance cameras, I could tell she had a lovely figure. My feelings about the ambassador's wife could not properly be called jealousy. What she inspired in me could more aptly be described as a sense of loss. She lived day to day with the elegant and serious ambassador, this man whom I had secretly come to care about. Despite the fact that I had never met him face to face, I had a feeling that we were matched in temperament, the ambassador and I, that in some complex way we were compatible. For all the good will I felt toward my husband, I could not say we were compatible.

The theater was already dark when I went in, and the ads were playing. A commercial for Hersheys came on, filling the air with the sweet, waxy smell of milk chocolate. Although the theater was crowded, there were still a few pairs of empty seats scattered about. I walked halfway to the back and took a seat at the very end of a row, on the left. I placed my handbag and coat in the empty seat next to me, hoping to deter anyone who might wish to sit there. Under my feet, I could feel the vibrations from the action adventure movie playing on the lower level. There were the usual trailers, followed by short ads for the theater's state-of-the-art sound and olfactory systems. Then the lights went down, a melancholy music began to play, and the scent of summer grass filled the air. An open field bathed in sunlight appeared on-screen. Then the camera moved out to reveal two children running through the field. It was strange to smell sun and grass when, outside, the weather was foggy and cold. Soon there was a kitchen on screen, a lonely housewife with a red kerchief around her head, the smell of baking bread.

"Excuse me," a voice said. For a moment I thought the voice had come from the speakers, but then I caught sight of a figure in the aisle on my left. "Is that seat taken?" he asked. I didn't look up to see his face, I just saw the hand with the popcorn gesturing at the seat next to me. Unhappily, I removed my coat and handbag from the empty seat and moved my legs aside as much as possible to allow the man to pass. Still, he could not help brushing the backs of his legs against my knees as he squeezed by. I looked up. His back was to me, a broad back in a woolen coat, and yet something about him seemed so familiar my breath caught in my throat.

He fumbled a bit getting into his seat, squeezed as it was between me and a rather large woman on the other side. Once he had sat down, I was able to see his face. It was the ambassador. He must have felt me looking at him, because he glanced over and gave me a little nod. I quickly turned my eyes toward the screen. A man had entered the dreary kitchen and was arguing with the woman. The music ended, and their voices rose and fell in a kind of domestic rancor. I was too startled to read the subtitles imposed in white over the ugly scene. The smell of the ambassador's popcorn mingled with the smell of baking bread from the movie, and I felt dizzy and a little nauseous.

I had always had the feeling that the ambassador rarely left the embassy, that he was trapped there in much the same way I was trapped in the house. But no, he was sitting beside me, flesh and blood. I could feel the heat from his body. If I dared put my hand on the armrest I might even touch his skin.

I spent the next two hours imagining possible scenarios, scripting each one in detail, with a beginning, middle, and end. Some of the scenarios involved only a few minutes, while others stretched on for years. All the while I felt the ambassador breathing beside me, heard the popcorn crunching between his teeth. He kept moving around, unable to get comfortable, and several times his leg brushed against my own.

Finally, the credits began to roll. The ambassador shifted in his seat, took his coat in his arms, but did not get up. He leaned forward to watch the credits. The theater began to empty. The credits went on and on. The emptier the theater became, the more strongly I felt the presence of the ambassador. Finally there was no one left but the two of us, sitting side by side in the dark. The final scene had been of a melancholy sexual encounter between the housewife and a bank manager, and the musky scent of sex lingered in the air, mingling with the ambassador's cologne, a strange, foreign fragrance. Added to these smells was a faint tinge of my own perspiration. The darkness of the theater, the closeness of our two bodies, the rows upon rows of empty seats, and the embarrassingly personal smells all combined to create an awkward intimacy.

By now the credits were finished, and he was obviously ready to leave. I gathered my handbag and coat and stepped into the aisle. I could hear him walking behind me. Moments later we were in the lobby. The next move came so easily, it felt as though I had been planning it all along. I had little to gain, much to lose, but what else could I do? I felt an acute sense of time passing, the remaining years moving rapidly toward an abrupt and unsatisfactory end.

I stopped and turned to face him. Our eyes were only inches apart. As the words formed in my mind, the hum began to grow fainter. "Mr. Ambassador," I said, and the choice seemed clear now, inevitable. He looked up. "I've seen you around the neighborhood," I blurted. "Would you like to have coffee?"

"Why not?" It took me a few seconds to register his response. Instead of my catching him off guard, it was the other way around.

We stepped outside, into the dim, foggy light. "I know a place just a few blocks from here," the ambassador said. I found myself being led by him along the crowded city street. It was a sensation at once thrilling and embarrassing; somehow, he had managed to put me in the role of an obedient child. As we walked, we talked very little. He made a comment about the weather, then pulled out his cell phone and checked his messages. He walked very fast, it was an effort to keep up. Eventually we arrived at a hole-in-the-wall sort of establishment, not a café but a bar. He glanced around before slipping inside the open door. There was no one in the place except the bartender, who looked up from the television and said to the ambassador, "I thought you'd disappeared."

"No, just busy," the ambassador replied. He walked to a little booth in a back corner, and not until we were seated did he finally put his cell phone away. He propped both elbows on the table and leaned forward, resting his chin on his folded hands. "Well," he said, smiling, "you obviously know who I am. Who are you?"

"Susan," I lied. Everything had happened so quickly and unexpectedly, it suddenly seemed wise not to divulge my real name.

"Jack and coke?" the bartender said, pulling a bottle off the shelf.

"Yes, and she'll have—" The ambassador paused, waiting for my response.

"A glass of pinot, please."

A radio station was playing over the speakers. The DJ had just come back from a commercial break and was announcing the call letters—KNBA, out of Anchorage, Alaska. "It's local appreciation hour," the DJ said. "Here's the Glacial Explosion, singing 'Time to Waste'."

The ambassador hummed along to the song. "The best way to judge a bar is by the music it plays," he said. "Roy knows his music."

Roy brought our drinks and returned to his stool behind the bar. A small overhead television was tuned to a soccer game.

The ambassador raised his glass in a toast. "To you, Susan."

Our glasses clinked. I didn't know where to go from there. Anything I'd ever wanted to say to him seemed inappropriate. The thrill of finally being eye to eye with the ambassador was somewhat tempered by the fact that it all seemed too easy, too quick. "I've seen you on TV," I said. "I've been keeping up with what's going on."

"Why?" He was looking at me with genuine surprise.

"Your country's been through a lot."

"It's a disaster," he said. "I talk and talk, but no one listens."

"At least you have your principles."

He stared at me with an amused expression. After all those months of observing him, I was the one who suddenly felt like a specimen under a microscope. "But you have something better," he said. With a sweep of his arm he indicated the open door, the world waiting outside. "You have this dream."

"What good is a corrupt dream?"

"A dream is always better than a nightmare."

He finished off his drink and ordered another, plus a second glass of wine for me. I had only taken a few sips of my first glass, but, feeling the need for courage, I quickly emptied it. Over the next hour, the ambassador asked me questions about my job, my background, and finally my family. "I suppose you have a husband," he said.

By now I was finishing my third glass of wine. "I do."

"I suppose you will not be telling the husband about this afternoon."

"I don't see how we've done anything wrong," I said. I could feel my face getting hot. The ambassador seemed to be enjoying my discomfort.

"True, but we both know we're about to," he said. "Let's go."

Part of me could not believe his directness, his lack of diplomacy. Another part of me understood that his steady gaze and unembarrassed proposition were small-scale indiscretions, perfectly befitting a man who dared defy the most powerful government on the planet.

Just as easily as he had found the bar, he found a hotel, an old four-story building that had probably been elegant at one time. The brass fixtures in the lobby had lost their sheen, and the red carpet on the grand staircase was worn and faded. While he checked in I browsed the hotel's gift shop, which contained the usual postcards bearing picturesque photos of the river, the hills, the city skyline. I was feigning interest in the postcards when he came up behind me and put his hands on my shoulders. It was the first tender gesture he had made since we met, and I felt all my feelings flooding back—desire, affection, pity, even a strange sense of camaraderie. Looking back, I realize that I was not thinking of my husband at that moment;

in hindsight, this mental omission seems strange. After all, I had never been unfaithful before, and if my husband discovered my infidelity, the marriage would surely be over. At the time, however, I was thinking only of the ambassador, replaying once again in my imagination the preposterous scenarios I had charted out for us.

If the lobby was elegantly shabby, the room itself, on the third floor overlooking the alley, was unabashedly depressing. Judging from the fine layer of dust coating the wooden desk and yellow lampshade, it might have been months since anyone had stayed there. In a classier hotel the seventies-era furnishings might have been stylishly retro, but here they were simply out-of-date.

There was nothing astonishing about the encounter. We undressed and got into bed, we kissed and touched and made the appropriate encouraging sounds. But for all my fantasies, all my nights of fevered dreaming, the event itself lacked passion. He finished too soon and apologized, I assured him I did not mind, we watched a few minutes of news on the television, and then he fell asleep. I sat on the edge of the bed for several minutes, listening. Because the room was located at the back of the hotel, off the main street, there were not even the ordinary city sounds to intrude upon our privacy. The hum was gone, completely gone, and what I heard in its place was silence, but it was not a comforting silence. Instead, there was something distressing about the absence of sound. Watching him sleep, a pale, bloated figure beneath the sheets, I realized I wasn't going to tell him about the second bedroom.

As I was getting dressed to leave, the ambassador woke up. "I'll see myself out," I said, but he insisted on accompanying me. Perhaps it was a custom of his country to walk the mistress to the door, or maybe it was simply a tardy attempt at good manners. At any rate, I could not dissuade him.

On the way out, he insisted that we stop in the gift shop, where he browsed for a few minutes before settling on a paperback book entitled *Haunted City*. A hand-lettered index card on the display shelf noted that the hotel itself received mention on page 74. The ambassador asked the ancient woman behind the desk to gift-wrap the book, which she did sloppily, although it was clear she was giving it her best effort. He paid with wrinkled bills and handed the package to me. I wasn't sure how he intended it to be received. Was it a parting gift? Was it some sort of consolation prize?

Just outside the door of the hotel he asked, "Which way are you going?"

I pointed toward the harbor. "You?" I asked.

To my relief, he nodded in the opposite direction.

After that, I ended my nightly trips to the garden. When I did venture out, it was always in some sort of disguise—with a scarf wrapped around my face, or in a bulky hat. Occasionally, I saw him in the window, but never again would I perceive him as I had on that first night, when he looked the picture of a noble man, principled and brave.

Every now and then, his country made some small blip in the news, most notably when the prime minister was ousted by a military coup. In the home that was not really a home, the machines kept humming. I did nothing to stop them. For weeks after our encounter, I lived in fear that I was being watched, that someone knew what I had done. But my indiscretions—the key, the breach of the second bedroom, the afternoon with the ambassador in the hotel—apparently went unnoticed. My husband and I lived there for another year before receiving the news that our services were no longer needed. By then we had saved enough money to buy a place of our own. My final act in the house was to open the drawer in the kitchen and make sure the key was in its proper place. I added a spot of glue to the contact paper in order to secure it firmly to the wood.

Not long ago I saw the ambassador on TV, reporting for a cable news network where he had taken a job as an international correspondent. He was in the capital of Urada. The buildings behind him were pockmarked with bullet holes. "I am standing on the site of the latest bloody battle between the new military government and the soldiers of the old guard," he said. His report showed no bias, no emotion, no despair, and I could not help but wonder how I could have been so singularly wrong in my initial judgment of him. I turned off the sound and watched the former ambassador. I was mesmerized even then by his blue eyes, the elegant scar across his nose. The report went on for another five minutes or so, during which time I tried and failed to recall the ambassador—not as he was, but as I had dreamt him to be.

MEDICINE

Once on the N-Judah train. Twice on BART. Three times in a stranger's car traveling toward Los Altos, where rows of burnt houses are waiting. Fifteen times in the living room of her small flat in the Richmond, with friends and casual acquaintances who had agreed to help. And each time she repeats a mantra she learned from her piano teacher twenty years ago, *Practice is the key to success.*

Really, it is not unlike any other task requiring manual dexterity. She is studying to get her license. The study is self-directed but the licenses are one hundred percent official and distributed by the health department. Prescription drugs are expensive these days, the Canadian border has been closed, progressive health departments are rapidly moving toward a concept of nurture over narcotics. The medically administered hand job has

become a common treatment for a number of non-terminal ill-
nesses:

- Heart arrhythmia
- Asthma
- Tendonitis
- Premature male-pattern baldness
- Back pain
- Near-sightedness
- Far-sightedness
- Depression
- Partial paralysis
- Hypertension

Surprisingly, the most obvious ailments are never treated
in this manner. Men with sexual malfunction, testicular cancer,
herpes, and urinary tract infections are forced to go the tra-
ditional route. In a new crop of informative medical journals
geared sympathetically toward the layperson, hand jobs are referred to as a "through the back door" method. Heal the cock,
and the heart/mind/knee/spine will follow.

Pulling earnestly on the fleshy stub of one arthritic Mr. Delfoy, the wheels of the N-Judah going round-round-round like a
song she remembers from Kindergarten, she notices that Mr.
Delfoy's fingers are gripping his briefcase with strength and agil-
ity. *Is he really even arthritic?* she wonders, as the N-Judah comes to
a halt in front of a rowdy schoolyard. Mr. Delfoy answered her
ad in the paper calling for courteous, professional, middle-aged
males to help her study for her exam. She met him at the agreed-
upon time at the bus stop at 20th and Lincoln. They exchanged
polite introductions, then boarded the bus together. Now that
it is a medically accepted practice, no more or less controversial

than doctor-prescribed marijuana, one often sees people engaging quietly in the treatment in public places, although some degree of discretion is expected. This time, for example, the patient laid his jacket over his lap before she commenced with the procedure. Mr. Delfoy lets go of the case, she lets go of him and wipes her hand on a napkin. The entire transaction, from initial meeting to completion, has taken less than ten minutes.

She recognizes, of course, that the system harbors great potential for abuse.

***

Not long ago, she worked as a copywriter for a small PR firm. Her career change was precipitated by a tragic event.

In Los Altos last month, wildfires swept in during a dry spell. Multi-million dollar homes in the hills, burning. Her own sister trapped up there, just seventeen and probably painting her nails or doing homework when she saw the flames approaching. Unlike the other twelve, her sister didn't die of smoke inhalation. With the first floor of the house already ablaze, she jumped out the third-floor window just moments before the fire truck arrived. "She would have made it," one fireman said, shaking his head, toeing the ground with a sneaker. He said this at a picnic in the park, a charity event for the victims. "We were *so close.*" He pulled a thin slice of pickle off his burger and dropped it on the ground.

Her sister did not break a single bone, but she hit her head on the garden's decorative brick border. The hardy geraniums survived.

Even as her sister was being carried away on a stretcher, the hoses were uncoiled, the mighty house was saved. Inside the house on the second floor were two live cats, one live dog, a school of exotic saltwater fish making their rounds in the giant aquarium. Outside, there was one dead sister. It was so like her to go gracefully—nothing broken, nothing bruised, not even a cut on the skull. But inside her head where mathematics had beautifully ruled, where equations and logarithms filled the intricate mazes, inside that lovely head the shoe-in for valedictorian, the good daughter, the baby sister, bled and bled and bled.

***

The licensing exam is in three parts: written, oral, and manual. The written is mostly multiple choice, with a couple of short answer questions thrown in to weed out the blatantly stupid.

Oral is the bedside manner portion of the exam, and it is strictly hands-off. The student sits face-to-face with a test subject, who reads from a script. A panel of examiners watches from behind a two-way glass. The test subject says things like, "I have been experiencing sharp shooting pains in my right calf," or "My doctor prescribed this treatment for migraines." The examinee then explains to the test subject what she is going to do, and how it is going to help him. Every now and then, the test subject will throw in a question or comment fraught with emotional landmines. This is where about twenty percent of potential licensees fail the examination. For example, the test subject might say, "I want you to take off your shirt," or "If you fuck me, no one will know." A skilled practitioner of the art will dismiss these comments in a polite but professional manner. A weaker examinee will become angry or flustered or, worse, flirtatious.

***

During the wake, a man she had never seen before walked up to the casket. This man put his hands on her dead sister's face, and he stood there for a long time and cried. After a while the family members became uncomfortable. She was delegated the task of removing the weeping stranger from the casket. She went up and stood beside him. His hands on her sister's face were very small. He was wearing a wedding ring.

"Excuse me," she said. He looked up. His eyes were red, his short black beard streaked with tears. "We haven't met," she said, feeling ridiculous. "She was my sister."

"Oh," he said. "Your sister took a summer course in astronomy I taught at the university." He glanced around at the crowd of mourners waiting for their turn at the casket. "She didn't mention me, did she?"

For a moment she deliberated. She looked at his small hands, his short beard, the hopefulness in his eyes. "As a matter of fact, she did. She said you were a very good teacher."

"Thank you," the man said, wiping his eyes with the back of his sleeve.

***

An interesting fact: while the ranks of general practitioner nurses remain primarily female, the new specialty in manual manipulation attracts mainly males. She learned this on CNN, in a heated debate between a well-known Democratic senator who supports medicinal hand jobs and the president of the American Family Coalition. The latter said, "God will strike America down like Sodom and Gomorrah if this is allowed to continue!" It was later revealed that the president of the AFC and his entire senior staff had been receiving treatments at a less-than-reputable clinic in Montgomery, Alabama, for going on two years.

Another interesting fact: the test subjects used in the examinations are never, ever average. They are either devastatingly sexy or monstrously ugly, the intention being to detect and discard two unworthy segments of the applicant pool: those of questionable morals and those lacking in compassion. She hopes she will get an ugly test subject. In this world, she is susceptible to two things: captive elephants and good-looking men. She has been known to make self-destructive sacrifices for members of both species. Her last boyfriend, for example, was six-foot-four and worked part-time as a hand model. It was for him that she moved into an Airstream Trailer in Pacifica, for him that she cut her hair short and took up vegetarianism.

***

The last time she saw her sister was at the Albertson's on California Street. They ran into each other at the checkout. Her sister had been busy with high school, she had been busy with her job at the PR firm, they had not seen each other in almost a month. They had always liked each other but had never been very close, because there were fifteen years between them.

"What are you doing in the city?" she asked.

"Just errands," her sister said, blatantly evading the question. Errands? In the city? So many miles from Los Altos? Her sister's shopping cart was stocked with small, expensive items, as if she were planning a gourmet meal. She placed a couple of rib-eye steaks on the conveyer belt, a small bag of fresh basil, some shitake mushrooms. "Mom wants you to come over for dinner soon."

"I know, I've been busy."

"Next Saturday?" her sister asked.

"Next Saturday, I promise."

"There's someone I want you to meet."

The thing she remembers most vividly from that encounter

is that her sister was wearing a pair of red brocade house slippers. Her sister, who was 5'2" and had been wearing platforms since she was thirteen, was shopping in public in house slippers. And she looked radiant, as if she'd just returned from an exotic vacation or received some very good news.

Three days later, her sister was dead. Only after the funeral did it occur to her that the person her sister wanted her to meet might have been the astronomy professor, and that the Albertson's on California Street was just a few blocks from the campus where he taught.

Ever since her sister died, she has felt a profound sense of disconnection—from her family, her work, the entire world. A few days after the funeral, she gave her two-weeks notice at the PR firm. "Why?" her boss said. He was wearing a post-it with a cartoon drawing of a Neanderthal man on his forehead, trying to make her laugh. Everyone in the office was trying to make her laugh.

"I need to find work that is more fulfilling," she said. She had rehearsed this line a number of times. Her boss came forward and hugged her.

"Tell me if there's anything I can do," he said. She could feel his steamy breath on her neck. The post-it bristled against her hair. For years the boss had tried unsuccessfully to hide his crush on her. Later, he would be one of the friends whom she called upon to help her prepare for the exam. She practiced on him three times: once behind the fly-fishing ponds in Golden Gate Park, once in his car, once in his light-filled loft in Potrero Hill. That was the time they ended up going to bed together. Afterward, he stroked her back and said, "Now that we're together, I can't let you pursue this career path."

"What?"

"I don't feel comfortable about you getting so intimate with other men."

"We're not together," she said. She got up and dressed, found her purse, her cell phone, her keys.

Naked, he followed her around the apartment. "Don't leave," he said. He tried the post-it trick again. She hasn't seen him since.

***

She is not the kind of person to make career decisions without thoroughly thinking them through. She did not quit her job at the PR firm without first considering the consequences. These factors drove her decision:

- Manual Manipulation is a booming and lucrative industry.
- The hours are flexible.
- She is not and never has been squeamish about bodily fluids.
- The male sexual organ is an organ like any other, in most instances not something to be feared or reviled. Erections and the male orgasm are mere reflexes, somewhat on par with knee-jerks and sneezing.
- She cannot remember the last time she did something even remotely selfless for another human being. She cannot remember the last time she touched another person in a way that felt truly intimate.

***

The portion of the exam about which she is most nervous is the manual. This is where fifty-seven percent of applicants flunk out. After a failure, one cannot sit for the exam again until thirteen months have passed. It is unclear where this time frame originated, but she suspects it is meant to weed out dilettantes. Thirteen months is plenty of time to find a new career path or to begin dating someone who doesn't approve, someone who puts his or her foot down.

She plans to pass the first time. At this point in her life there is no other career path, no potential love waiting in the wings. The boss is not on her radar. All of her exes have swiftly and cruelly moved on. She realizes from past breakups that she is an easy person with whom to sever ties. She is thirty-two. Her last boyfriend married a software executive and is living in a two-million-dollar bungalow in Palo Alto. Recently on the phone the ex said to her, "I am flush with love and cash," and there was no hint of self-deprecation in his voice. The software executive is expecting.

"Expecting what?" she said when the ex told her the news.

"You know," he said, sighing the exasperated sigh that characterized most of their exchanges during the final year of their relationship. "Expecting."

"But you said you never wanted children," she reminded him. "You said children have nothing to offer. You said they would cause undue wear on your hands. The diapers, remember? The preparation of nutritious meals. The assembling of swing sets."

To which he replied, "You always were so negative."

***

The week after the funeral she received a call from the astronomy professor. He was weeping. "I have to see you," he said. "I need to talk to someone."

They met at the diner by Lake Merced. It was a cool day, college students were rowing through the fog on the lake. The afternoon special was chicken salad on rye served with a side of hash browns. She had the special, he had coffee, he confessed he had been deeply in love with her sister.

"My sister was only seventeen," she said. "You're a married man."

His eyes were so small, his hands so small, his beard so short and bristly, she wondered what her beautiful sister could possibly have seen in him.

"Did you know her dream was to map the distance between Earth and the nearest sentient life-forms outside our solar system? Yes, she was young, but she was working on a mathematical formula that could quite possibly have changed the way humans view our place in the universe."

She looked at her hash browns and shook her head dumbly. "No, I didn't know."

"What I'm saying is, to you she was a seventeen-year-old girl. To me she was a great scientist in the making."

And a lover, she wanted to add. *And you're married.* But she didn't say it. It occurred to her that perhaps her sister had tapped into something good but indefinable—a kind of connection that she herself was still waiting to experience.

***

Although a number of schools have opened to serve the vast number of hopefuls flocking to the new profession, formal training is not required to sit for the exam. Nonetheless, she briefly considered enrolling in a local certificate program in order to validate the respectability of her chosen path, but when she looked into it she discovered the costs would be prohibitive. Three thousand dollars per semester, and that didn't even include the lubricant.

Anyway, what she knows about hand jobs could fill a text-book. She gave her first at fourteen, to a banker's son named John Zephyr, in the living room of her friend Ramona's house during a party at which no adults were present. Everyone had been drinking Seagram's and Seven, and John Zephyr was passed out on the sofa. Someone sent her to wake him up, it was long past his curfew. She tried slapping his face, pulling his hair, talking loudly into his ear, but he just kept on snoring.

Then she saw that his pants were unzipped, a fact that was not entirely surprising given the haze of marijuana and alcohol that wafted through the house. She opened the fly of his boxers and gently took him in her hands. She had not planned on doing it; it just happened that way. Soon he was awake and proclaiming his undying love. She was surprised by the pleasant stiffness in her hands, and the way this boy who had paid no attention to her before succumbed entirely to her control.

After that, she was very popular at parties.

When she tells the ex about her new direction, he says, "You always were good at *that*." He has a way of turning every compliment into a stinging insult, just by his tone of voice.

***

Sometimes she lies awake late into the night, thinking of her sister. The image is always the same: her sister stepping up on the windowsill, looking back one last time at her bedroom. The woods around her blaze with firelight. In her brilliant mind, she calculates the distance from windowsill to ground. She considers the probabilities of her survival. The ground beneath her window is soft, the first floor of her house is burning, it only takes a few seconds to die of smoke inhalation. For some reason, she does not factor in the brand-new brick border framing the geraniums.

***

When people ask why a nice copywriter like herself is making such a dramatic career shift, she mentions the good pay, the flexible hours, the geographic mobility. She does not mention that she has always been at ease when giving a hand job. She never admits that she finds it comforting, the feel of her palm against giving flesh, the way she can control a man's face and his emotions with a simple shift in speed or rhythm. She doesn't say that she enjoys the moment of intense tightening just before he lets go, and then the quick, hot stream of semen. She never mentions these things because she fears that perhaps she is a little strange, to find peace and wholeness in such a simple, primal act.

And she tells no one what goes through her mind while she is working on her practice subjects. Occasionally, she tries to concentrate on rhythm and technique, speed and accuracy. More often, though, her mind wanders, and she finds herself thinking about everything except the job at hand:

- Will she see her ex, the software engineer, and their new baby on the street? If so, what will she say?
- If, on that day at Albertson's, she had known she were seeing her sister for the last time, what would she have said?
- Did her sister believe in an afterlife? Does she herself believe in an afterlife? If there is an afterlife, will she one day in the distant future be able to locate her sister there?
- How do her parents manage to pass the endless days in that enormous, immaculate house in the Los Altos hills, and does her mother still tend the geraniums?

***

The day of the exam arrives. She goes to a nondescript building on Polk Street, rides the elevator to the twelfth floor, and joins thirty-seven other hopefuls for the written exam. She uses a number two pencil and finishes half an hour early, certain that she has aced it.

The oral exam is more difficult. Her test subject is extremely attractive. She resorts to an old technique she has of slightly crossing her eyes in order to blur her vision. This way, she does not have to look at his beautiful green eyes, his perfect face. He reads from his script in a convincing way. When he says, "I'm so ashamed to be here," she says, "There is nothing to be ashamed of. This procedure is a medically sound method of relieving upper back pain." A few minutes later, following the script, he says, "You fucking whore," to which she replies, "Please refrain from making comments which may interfere with the treatment." As she is leaving the room, she can hear murmurs behind the two-way glass. She spends half an hour in the waiting room, flipping through *Popular Mechanics*.

Finally, the administrative assistant calls her name and says, "Please proceed to room 1237 for the manual portion of your exam."

She finds her test subject in a large room containing nothing but two hard-backed chairs. The room is painted white. To her great relief, the test subject is a fat man in his mid-fifties with a receding hairline, complaining of excruciating leg cramps. She takes a pair of disposable surgical gloves from a box by her chair and gets to work. It only takes three minutes and twenty-seven seconds.

The next day she receives her final results by phone. A sleepy voice of indiscriminate sex says: "We are calling to inform you that you have passed all three segments of the Manual Medical

Caregiver examination. You were in the top third percentile of your exam group. Congratulations, this is the beginning of an exciting new career in medicine."

***

A few weeks after she passes the exam, her mother calls and says, "You never came to dinner."

Meaning, of course, that she is a lousy daughter, that she quite possibly caused the fire, that it should have been she who died instead of her younger sister.

Her mother says, "Your father wants to talk to you."

Her father comes on the line. "Who is this?"

"It's me."

"Oh, hello, I heard through the grapevine that you've become one of those whatchamacallits."

"Manual Medical Caregiver."

"Yes, how do you like the work?"

"It's good, not too stressful, it pays the bills."

She can hear her mother whispering something in the background. "Sweetheart," her father says. "Your mother wants you to return the necklace you borrowed from your little sister."

"What necklace?"

More whispering, then, "The one with the rhinestone rhinoceros pendant."

She has to think for a minute, and then she remembers it. "That was five years ago."

Her father sighs. It has been a long and arduous marriage. She knows this for a fact: he never wanted children. He never even wanted a wife. Before he got her mother pregnant, he'd been planning a solitary career in forestry. "Your mother wants it back," her father says. "I can't say why. Just do this one thing for the sake of harmony."

"Sure," she says.

Months pass. She never finds the necklace, she never goes over for dinner. She cannot bear the thought of her mother's cautious hug, the polite pat on the shoulder, the inevitable point in the evening when her mother would remind her, "Your sister took after me, you know. You're the spitting image of your father." After dinner she would help her father in the kitchen, while her mother retired to her sister's bedroom, which is where she sleeps these days.

She advertises her services on the back page of a reputable local magazine and gradually builds her clientele. She rents a small office in the financial district. The office contains a couch, a chair, a pillow, a desk on which she makes appointments and keeps the books. She paints the walls a pale, hospitable blue and maintains a large supply of Kleenex. She always wears scrubs to work, in order to underscore the message to patients that this is a serious medical establishment. She finds the work relaxing. She sleeps fairly well at night. Her patients depend on her, she is providing a valuable service to the public. Slowly, she begins to feel connected to the world.

But there is one thing that bothers her, one horror she can't shake: the image of her baby sister standing on the windowsill, preparing to leap. She purchases several books about the afterlife. Each night before falling asleep, she attempts unsuccessfully to channel her sister's ghost.

***

Oh yes, of course it happens this way. She runs into the ex on the street. He is pushing a stroller, and the software executive is beaming. The software executive has gotten a perm and a thousand-dollar pram. "I quit my job!" this woman says, unprovoked. "Motherhood is so fulfilling!"

Consequently, the ex has taken a full-time job for the first time in his life. He has given up his career in hand modeling for something more stable, something in sales. He looks haggard, possibly insane, and she knows he is ready to jump ship at any moment. When the software executive runs off to change the baby's diaper, the ex says, "Would you like to have coffee sometime?"

"I don't think so." She does not even feel the slightest emotional tug, the slimmest pang of nostalgia-lust.

One thing she never told anyone about her ex: he did not masturbate. Ever. He was concerned about repetitive stress injury to his hands.

***

Nearly a year after she passes the exam, the astronomer shows up at her door. It's late on a rainy night, and she's wearing her nightgown, watching old Westerns on TV. She has not seen him since that day at the diner.

"May I come in?" he asks.

He is wearing a yellow raincoat in which he looks very small, no bigger than a boy. She steps aside to let him in. She offers him coffee and a bagel. Still wearing his wet raincoat, he sits down on the sofa. She sits on the other end. His face has the gaunt, prematurely aged look of someone who has given up food for cigarettes.

"I can't get her out of my mind," he says.

"I know," she says. By which she means, "Me too."

"I've left my wife," he says. "I've quit my job. I've been spending a lot of time at sports bars."

She is thinking about her sister, how one young girl with an infinite stream of numbers coursing through her brain could have caused so much grief for so many people simply by ceasing to exist. She doesn't know what to say to him, so she tells him a story that she only recently remembered.

"I remember this one time," she says. "My sister was six years old, and I was home from college. It was 1986, and Haley's comet was passing by. She'd heard about it in school, and she was desperate to see it. I drove her out to Pt. Reyes, and we camped out on the beach. I remember it was this bright baseball of light with a fuzzy white tail. We lay on our backs, watching. My sister took a few pictures with a Polaroid camera, but none of them came out. When I woke up the next morning she was sitting down by the water's edge. I asked her what she thought of the comet. 'It was cool,' she said. Then she asked me the strangest thing. 'How far away do you think they are?' she asked. 'Who?' 'The other people,' she said. 'How many light-years do you think it would take to get to the nearest planet inhabited by people?' I said I didn't know, but there'd be plenty of time for her to figure it out."

The astronomer is looking at her with extreme concentration, as if waiting for some clue, some consoling fact, that will allow him to get on with his life. "Yes, I remember when Haley's comet passed by," he says. "Do you know it won't return until the year 2061?"

They sit for a few minutes in silence. John Wayne's voice emanates softly from the TV.

Finally she says, "Why are you here?"

He leans his wet head against the sofa. "I don't know."

It occurs to her that she need not let him suffer. It occurs to her that he has come to her for a purpose, even if he is unaware of this himself.

"I am a licensed medical professional," she says, sliding closer to him. "Manual manipulation has proven extremely effective in treating patients who suffer from long-term mourning." She is using her most professional voice. She touches his hand first, in keeping with protocol. He flinches slightly, but does not move his hand away.

He lifts his head and looks at her. "It's very kind of you, but I don't think that will help. Nothing will help." His hair is dripping on her sofa.

"At least we can try," she says. "I won't charge you."

"Okay."

She goes upstairs, puts on her scrubs, and gets a bottle of lotion. When she returns, he has taken off his raincoat and laid it over the arm of the sofa. He has unzipped his pants and is sitting with his hands in his lap. "What now?" he asks nervously.

"Just relax."

She reaches for him and begins to work. He is so soft, so small. As she is working, she thinks about the universe. She thinks about planets spinning. She sees cold moons and burning suns. She thinks about the year 2061, and she is pleased by the thought that, when the comet passes again, she too will be nothing more than particulate matter.

Soon, the astronomer shudders and lets out a great sigh. He opens his eyes and says, "Elizabeth." For a moment she forgets the rules and leaves her hand in place. For a moment she is not alone in the world, she is connected to some greater thing. It is the first time she has heard her sister's name spoken aloud in many months.

LAKE

I was in Golden Gate Park watching the gentlemen race their model yachts on Spreckels Lake. I used to go there a lot to take my mind off things. The scene was always the same: a dozen or so men in their seventies, eighties, even nineties, decked out in fishing caps and khakis and sneakers, pacing the sidewalk, remote controls in hand. The men were always in a hurry, scurrying to keep up with their yachts, but the yachts themselves never went very fast. The yachts were so slow, in fact, not even the ducks seemed to be bothered by them.

It was a small lake, man-made and gracefully shaped, seductively curvaceous like the amoebae one studies in grade school. The lake was surrounded by a wide sidewalk. Along the edges of the sidewalk were several wooden benches with little brass dedication plaques *in loving memory of* this or that person; there was even a bench devoted to someone's cat. The character of the lake changed from day to day, depending on the weather. On this particular afternoon the placid surface was covered with a thin green film.

There was a new guy at the lake. He was tall and broad, probably not a day over 65. His boat was brand new, bigger than the others, with a showy red hull beneath the billowing white sail. He was very tan, as if he'd spent the last twenty years of his life in Florida, and he wore a blue baseball cap instead of the regulation fishing hat. He was being aggressive, pulling all sorts of bogus maneuvers. At one point he swung his yacht around and slammed into a smaller one that was attempting to pass.

"Please get that monstrosity out of the way," said the fellow with the smaller boat. He had an old-fashioned mustache and dyed black hair, and he wore an odd pair of white gloves with pearl buttons at the wrists. Every time I went to Spreckels Lake—I'd been going twice a week for several months, ever since my husband left—this fellow was there. He had always struck me as meek, so I was surprised to hear him challenge the new guy.

"What did you say?" the new guy asked.

"This is a gentleman's sport," the fellow with the white gloves replied. "There is a protocol. Kindly move your boat."

That's when the new guy said, "Fuck off," and pushed the gentlemanly fellow into the lake.

The man disappeared beneath the water for a few seconds. Then his head bobbed up, his knees, the white tips of his shoes, and he began to float.

As soon as the men of the model yacht club realized what had happened, they started steering their boats in and calling out for help, everyone except the new guy, who apparently still had his sights set on winning the race.

By now the fellow had floated several yards out. "Should someone go in to help him?" one man asked. The others shrugged their shoulders. I got the feeling none of them went in for much physical activity. Plus, the water was green and slimy. I was the only other person at the lake, so they all looked my way, but they quickly dismissed me, because I was obviously very pregnant. Thirty-eight weeks, to be exact. Two weeks to go, give or take. I was in no condition to jump into the lake and save the floating man. We all just stood there for a moment, trying to figure out what to do. It was clear that no one else had a cell phone or a rescue plan.

Gradually the men began taking their boats out of the water and drying them off in their careful, tender way. I could tell they were disappointed, but they couldn't very well go on racing their boats while one of their own was in a dire situation. The new guy pulled his yacht past the finish line and yelled, "I won!" but no one paid him any attention.

"Why don't you jump in there and save him?" I said to the new guy. "After all, you're the one who pushed him in."

"I did no such thing," the new guy said, pulling his baseball cap low on his forehead and frowning at me in a threatening way. He probably would have pushed me in too if I hadn't been so pregnant. He looked around furtively, then took his monster yacht out of the water and walked away.

The fellow in the lake, who had drifted out about fifteen yards, said, "Might someone lend me a hand?"

"Can you swim?" asked one of the men of the model yacht club.

This seemed to strike the fellow with the white gloves as a novel notion. "I've never tried."

Someone else offered, "This isn't the time to find out. Just float. The human body can float for an indefinite period of time. The key is to relax. The moment you panic, you sink."

"You could try standing up," said a man with a tattoo of an eagle sprawled across his right arm. "It may not be very deep."

"What if it is?" asked the floating man.

"You're right," another man said. "The safest bet is to just keep floating until something happens."

The men of the model yacht club deliberated for a minute, and finally agreed that yes, floating was the safest option. So we stood and watched as the gentlemanly fellow drifted farther away from us. In his plaid shirt, bright white sneakers, and white gloves, he looked like some unlikely freshwater creature hailing from another world.

"How long do you think it will be before the situation improves?" the floating man asked. I detected a note of concern in his voice, but overall I thought he was being very dignified about the whole thing.

"Don't worry," I called. "We'll wait here until you float to the edge or until help arrives." I was surprised to hear my own voice. I wasn't in the yacht club, after all. If I wanted to, I could simply walk away.

"Who was that?" asked the floating man.

The men of the yacht club looked at me. "It was the pregnant lady," said one. He uttered the word *pregnant* in a whisper, as if it were some divine condition deserving of respect.

"Oh, of course, I've seen you here many times. How are you feeling?"

"Fine."

"Is it a boy or a girl?"

"A boy."

"That's wonderful," the floating man said. "I have three grandsons myself."

We all sat down and waited, making conversation with the floating man.

"It's only a matter of patience," someone called out to him. "By and by you'll float back over this way, and we'll pull you out."

"I'd appreciate that."

"Just concentrate," said a man who was wearing very yellow socks.

"On what?" came the reply from the middle of the lake.

"On your favorite food or a beautiful girl you had a very long time ago." The man in the yellow socks glanced at me. "Sorry, I'm just trying to help him focus."

"No offense taken."

It was a funny thing about being pregnant, everyone just assumed that I was both physically and emotionally delicate, not to mention prudish. In the weeks before my husband left, he had become solicitous, plumping my pillows at night and fetching things from the kitchen, holding on to my arm when we walked as if I might trip and fall at any moment. Although the hormonal changes made me lustier than usual, he refused to have sex with me, convinced he would harm the baby or me. He even tried to stop cursing, and when he slipped up he would apologize profusely.

The gentleman continued to float. The sun went behind the clouds. No one came by. It was just us out there—me and the old guys and the floating man, and the wildlife, of course. The lake was a gathering place for fowl of many varieties, and I was always amazed at how well they got along: the pesky pigeons with their drugged-looking red eyes, the mallards with their emerald necks, the seagulls with black and white tail feathers resembling piano keys. A pigeon was resting on the floating man's stomach and a black baby duck was perched on his forehead. It was all very peaceful.

As I sat there I began to think about my grandfather, who had been known throughout the Southeast decades before as The Great Amphibian. He earned this title by way of a special talent he had for disappearing into the water and reappearing hours later, completely unharmed. The first person to witness this particular feat was the girl who would become my grandmother. She was a student at Wesleyan College in Macon, Georgia, at the time, and she was rowing with her roommate on Foster Lake when she spotted an attractive man in his early twenties on the far side of the lake. He waved to her. She waved back.

"I'm coming out there," he shouted.

"Don't," she said, "it's deep. We'll come to you."

Then he stepped into the lake.

The strange thing was that he did not swim, he just stepped in and started walking. He was wearing all of his clothes—a seersucker suit with a white shirt and pale blue tie. His knees disappeared, his waist, his chest, his neck, and finally his head. She and her roommate thought it was a nifty trick until more than a minute passed, and he did not emerge. They scanned the lake and saw no sign of him. There weren't any bubbles or ripples on the surface to indicate where he might be. They began to row in the direction where he'd been standing, but neither girl was skilled with the paddle and they ended up going in circles. My grandmother went into a panic, thinking she had just witnessed a drowning. Then, about seven and a half minutes after he had stepped into the lake, my grandfather bobbed up beside their boat.

"Hello," he said.

His head rose so calmly over the surface of the water that he did not even seem to be moving his hands or feet. It was the strangest thing my grandmother had ever seen, and that very moment she fell in love. He climbed into the boat and shared the girls' picnic lunch. Seventeen days later, the wedding ceremony was held on the front lawn of the campus. My grandmother begged her new husband to reveal the secret of how he had disappeared into the lake for seven and a half minutes without coming up for air, but he only said, "Most folks put too much store by oxygen."

Ten months later they had a son—my father—and soon after the birth my grandfather lost his job. Deciding that her husband should put his aquatic talents to use for financial gain, my grandmother started printing flyers and calling friends, one of whom wrote a column for the *Macon Star*. On my father's six-month birthday, twenty-nine skeptics showed up on the banks of Foster Lake, deposited a quarter into a cookie tin my grandmother had brought along for the occasion, and waited to see my grandfather walk into the water. The promise made in the newspaper column and on the flyers was that he would stay underwater for six minutes without coming up for air, but he astonished everyone by staying under for nine minutes and forty-seven seconds. He repeated the trick for a larger audience a week later, only this time he made a different promise: he would walk all the way from one side of the lake to the other. It took thirteen minutes and twelve seconds; when he emerged on the other side a newspaper photographer took his picture. In the photograph my grandfather is wearing a seersucker suit and pale tie which hang dripping from his body—likely the same suit and tie he wore on the day he met my grandmother—and his hair is slicked away from his face. He is smiling. The headline above the photograph reads, simply, "The Great Amphibian." Thus he embarked upon a lucrative new career.

"How do you do it?" a reporter once asked. My grandfather is said to have tipped his hat and replied, "It's simple, really. I just put one foot in front of the other."

I never knew my grandfather, because he disappeared before I was born. But as a child I often heard about him. My father would always tell the story with a sort of awe, and after my father left my mother began telling it. I think both of them wanted me to know that I had greatness in my blood, that the path leading to my birth was paved with golden sand. "The water was his calling," my father used to say, rocking me in the big white chair by the window overlooking the wharf. "What is yours?"

I never knew how to answer the question; I felt called to nothing, by no one, and I feared that I would live out my days without knowing my true purpose.

From my bedroom window in those days I could see the bay, stretching out cool and blue, and the swaybacked length of the Golden Gate Bridge, half obscured by fog, and far in the distance the lonely island of Alcatraz. I knew that my grandfather had always dreamed of walking underwater the entire distance from San Francisco to Alcatraz. He had tried several times, and failed. In the family album there was a newspaper photo of him being rescued from the frigid bay waters by a Coast Guard boat, just three tenths of a mile from his goal. According to my parents, it was a failure that he always regretted, and though in his lifetime he walked hundreds of miles beneath dozens of bodies of water in all kinds of weather, he always saw San Francisco Bay as his great defeat.

The legend was that my grandfather had met some dire fate in Lake Michigan during a family vacation, but there was no proof; his body was never recovered. Because no one could say for certain what had happened to him, I believed he could have gone anywhere, and he might very well still be alive. I imagined that he had returned at some point to San Francisco, that alone and without fanfare he had made the dangerous underwater trek to Alcatraz. As a child I spent many afternoons staring out the window at the bay and imagining my grandfather, The Great Amphibian, stepping into the frigid water, walking and walking until he came to that eerie, abandoned island. In my mind, he had finally succeeded—without an enraptured audience, without a fanatical wife to cheer him on. I imagined him living alone on the terrible island, roaming the empty prison cells, walking to the city whenever he became bored or lonely or needful of supplies. Sometimes, strolling along the crowded downtown streets hand in hand with my father—and later, after my father had left, alone—I would watch for a thin, graying man in a drenched seersucker suit. For many years, I believed without doubt that I would one day run into him in Union Square or along the waterfront, and that he would immediately recognize me as his own, blood of his blood, granddaughter of The Great Amphibian.

***

Hours passed. There was the sound of ducks squawking and the men of the model yacht club chatting and the cars passing on Fulton, beyond the line of trees. By and by everyone began to leave. One had to go teach an adult education art course at UC Berkeley Extension, another had a dinner party to attend, another had a grandchild to babysit. I, being single and on maternity leave from the law firm, was entirely without obligations, so I stayed.

It grew darker. Sometimes the floating man and I talked, and sometimes we remained silent, listening to the wind in the eucalyptus trees. No one came by the lake. The Giants were fighting their way to the playoffs at Pac-Bell Park, a presidential debate was being broadcast on TV, the Dalai Lama was giving a speech at Yerba Buena, Bruce Springsteen was playing at the Great American Music Hall. It was one of those San Francisco days when everyone had somewhere else to be, leaving the streets and parks deserted. I always liked San Francisco best on those days, because one had the feeling of living anonymously and alone in a great, unpopulated city.

"You can go home if you need to," the floating man said. I could tell he was just trying to be brave, he didn't really want to be left alone.

"That's okay. It's pleasant here."

"Won't your husband be worried?"

"He died," I said.

"My condolences."

I felt guilty for lying to the floating man, but it was so much easier to say my husband had died than to say he had simply departed. What a shock it had been the day I came home from work to find a note on the dining room table: "You and the baby will be better off without me." His leave-taking came without warning; there had been no foreshadowing, no aberrant behavior that appeared in retrospect as a series of telltale clues. I was four months along, and we were presumably happy. I waited for him to return, certain that he was simply afraid and would soon realize his mistake. A month passed, two, three, and gradually it began to seem inevitable. Of course he had left, of course I would raise this child alone, wasn't that in keeping with family tradition?

My grandfather, The Great Amphibian, had left his family, after all, just stepped into Lake Michigan one summer during a vacation to Chicago and started walking. My grandmother thought nothing of it, being used to his underwater escapades. She waited for him all morning, then through lunchtime and on into evening. By suppertime she had to pack up; the children were hungry and sunburned, the lake at night was no place for a respectable family. She and the children waited in their hotel room for a week and finally went home, immersed in the cold grief of uncertainty. Her husband was never heard from again. My father left my mother and me as well; a week after my tenth birthday he went on a business trip to Atlanta from which he did not return. His sister, my aunt, left her husband and three children for a career in dentistry. It was the way it went among our clan, and the trick was to be the one who left rather than the one who was left behind.

"How did it happen?" the floating man asked. "How did your husband die?"

"A tragic hunting accident," I said. It was the first thing that came to me.

For a while neither of us spoke.

At some point I checked my watch and saw that it was 8:15. The fog had moved in, shifting through the green treetops and hovering over the green lake. The air was cold. "How are you doing out there?" I asked.

"I've felt better."

"Is there anything I can do to help take your mind off things?"

"Tell me a story," he said. "A very long one."

So I told him the story of The Great Amphibian, how he became famous and made a good living for many years by going from state to state, lake to lake, walking underwater. I explained how my grandfather's celebrity earned him enough money to buy a house in Atlanta and another in San Francisco, where he tried and failed to walk to Alcatraz. I told the floating man about my grandfather's disappearance in Lake Michigan, and his strange reappearance some years later on page sixteen of the *Bay Guardian*. It was a small item in the News of the Weird column, and I would have missed the story altogether were it not for the intriguing subhead, printed in bold letters:

"Man or Fish?" I read the paragraph over and over so many times it was etched permanently into my memory:

Two campers from New York City whose fishing boat capsized in Big Moose Lake in the Adirondacks were rescued Friday by an unidentified man. The drunken campers were flailing about in the water when a fully clothed man appeared beside them in the middle of the lake and escorted them to safety. Following the rescue, the man bowed cordially and disappeared once again into the lake. A witness at the campsite corroborated their story. Both campers were treated for hypothermia at a nearby hospital and released.

When I saw this piece I was a junior in college, majoring in pre-law, and I had just met the man who would one day become my husband, a graduate student in musicology. My courtship with this tall, thin man who played saxophone and didn't own a car was the first thing that had ever struck me with the sort of intensity that might be described as a calling. Evenings, we would have burnt coffee and soggy hash browns at a diner in the Mission, and as I sat across from him, listening to his inspired rants on the roots of the blues, I felt as if my long years of indirection had finally come to an end.

What intrigued me most about the story in the *Bay Guardian* was the word "escorted," which implied a certain casual grace, very much in keeping with what I knew of my grandfather. The fact that the rescuer was fully clothed, combined with the strange circumstances of his departure from the campers, convinced me beyond doubt that The Great Amphibian was alive and well. Was he living somewhere along the banks of Big Moose Lake, or had he merely been visiting? Was he in New York State by chance, or had he taken up permanent residence there?

"That was eight years ago," I told the floating man. "For several months afterwards I tried to locate my grandfather. I called all the campsites around the lake, but no one knew a man who could walk underwater. Then I called directory assistance for every town and city in the state of New York, but there was no one listed by his name. Eventually I gave up."

At the end of my story I heard a strange sound coming from the middle of Spreckels Lake. The floating man was snoring. I checked my watch. It was almost nine p.m., I was hungry and I had to pee and I wanted to go home. I did not know what to do. I could not let the gentleman stay out there on the lake, floating through the night, but I could not leave him to find help. I realized that it was up to me to save him. But swimming was not my thing, I had never liked it. I remembered sitting on the steps of the shallow end of a dirty pool at Kinder Kare when I was six, refusing to get wet above the waist. For an entire summer, day after day, I ignored the exhortations of my teacher to go in. Finally, she told my mother that I could no longer attend classes, as I was demoralizing to the other children.

"A shame," my mother said to the teacher. "Her grandfather, of course, was known as The Great Amphibian."

Eventually I did learn to swim, but not by choice. It was at Girls in Action camp the summer before my sixth grade year. One afternoon two coconut-smelling counselors, one fat, one thin, picked me up by the arms and legs, carried me down to the end of the pier, and threw me in the water.

"Swim for Jesus," the thin girl yelled.

"He died on the cross for you," the fat girl said. "Can't you at least swim for him?"

I sputtered and dog paddled and gasped for air. I felt that I was dying. But eventually I did swim, not for Jesus but for Jordan Lamar, a member of the Royal Ambassadors who was watching from the desolate brown beach. Eventually I made it to shore. That was my first and last experience with swimming.

Sitting alone by Spreckels Lake in the quiet of the evening, watching the sleeping man float, I remembered a Girls in Action pamphlet entitled, "You too can be a hero." The pamphlet featured drawings of peach-skinned blonde girls committing heroic acts such as rescuing injured birds, helping old ladies cross the street, and witnessing to people who might otherwise go to hell. I had never done any of these things, and had ended my three years of Girls in Action without a single Hero Badge on my uniform. On the day of my Girls in Action commencement, my mother didn't even bring a camera. She cried throughout the ceremony while other women's daughters received accolades and gave speeches. In the car on the way home, she said, by way of subtle accusation, "Your grandfather, remember, was known as The Great Amphibian."

"Not everyone can be great."

I said this to provoke her, thinking that she would lecture me about how I *could* be great if only I weren't so lazy. Instead, she gave me a look that was painfully devoid of anger or confrontation and said, "I guess you're right. What say we go to Dairy Queen?" By that point my father had already gone AWOL, and my mother often plied me with unhealthy snacks in order to make up for his absence. At Dairy Queen I had a Peanut Butter Parfait. The crumbled peanuts were stale and the plastic spoon wouldn't reach all the way to the bottom of the cup. On that day I became resigned to a life of mediocrity, and over time I realized that mediocrity suited me well. I have a decent career. I live in a decent house. For a while, I was married to a decent man. Perhaps my parents had been wrong all along, and greatness was not, after all, genetic.

That night at the lake, it was not greatness I strove for. I did what I did out of fear—fear of leaving the floating man on the lake to go for help, only to come back and find him drowned and dead, fear of living with the consequences of my act of desertion. While I could abide old ladies crossing the street alone, injured birds dying in the woods, even the great unsaved masses going to hell, I could not abide the thought of that nice man from the model yacht club dying alone in the lake, abandoned by everyone.

I cannot say for sure why noble conviction struck me on this particular day, when I had lived my entire life without it. Perhaps some part of me did not want my unborn son to witness his mother in an act of cowardice. Whatever the reason, I took off my jacket and shoes, walked to the water's edge, sat down on the cool cement, and lowered myself into the lake.

The water was cold and slippery. A fine green film coated my feet, my calves, my thighs. The moment my stomach touched the water, my baby began to kick.

"I hear something," the floating man called. His voice was fearful, startled from sleep. "Is that you?"

"Yes," I shouted. "I'm coming to get you."

"Oh, thank heavens," he said. "I'm so cold."

"How did you sleep?" I asked, trying to take his mind off his situation.

"Oh, I didn't really sleep. I just dozed. That was a fine story you told about your grandfather. How ever did it end? Did you find him?"

"I'll tell you another day."

I didn't have the heart to tell him that I had already revealed the ending, and that he had slept right through it. Nor did I want to tell him that The Great Amphibian had never materialized, that after living three decades in the shadow of his greatness I had yet to meet him.

My feet touched the slimy cement bottom. I would be lying if I said I wasn't afraid, but it was a manageable fear. I decided to just put one foot in front of the other, as my grandfather had done for so many years, and see what happened. The water reached my chest, my shoulders, my neck. I could feel the baby beneath my ribs, could feel the strength of his tiny hands and feet. An elbow— or was it a knee?—traveled slowly across my stomach. At that moment I believed that he would be a fine baby, a good son, and the blood of The Great Amphibian would flow through his veins.

The water touched my chin, my mouth, my nose. I kept walking. I felt the water closing over the top of my head. Slowly, my lungs began to tighten, and in the tightness there was a kind of clarity, a vanishing of fear. I saw then that it was not so very far out to the middle of the lake. In the liquid darkness I could just make out the shape of the floating man—his legs, his arms, his gloved hands—sprawled and waiting.

HERO

I've been having these egg-headed thoughts about non-linear time and a parallel universe. I've been having these thoughts for twenty years, and lately they've been coming between me and my wife. My wife believes in one world, one time, one perfect moment. My wife believes in making the decision, because, she says, looking up from the PBS documentary *Life of Baby*, "right now is all we've got." I'm standing on the fire escape of our one-bedroom sublet at 85th and Columbus, working the grill, conversing with her through the open window. She's rubbing her belly in a wistful manner. There's this baby on the TV screen, newly delivered, a tiny glistening bundle, and my wife is looking at this baby like it's just about the most beautiful thing on the planet.

My wife defends murderers for a living, and she means it when she says that stuff about right now. One minute you're buying beaded purses from a vendor on 34th Street, and the next, poof, you're dead on the stairwell, skirt hiked above your knees, neck twisted in an unnatural way, a black cord around your throat, some guy's wet dream. Sometimes at night she brings her work home, spreads photographs of the victims across the kitchen table and studies them, trying to figure out why, given the evidence, her guy can't be connected beyond a shadow of a doubt to this particular body. Sometimes, out of grotesque curiosity, a fascination with the horror that is my wife's bread and butter, I glance at the photos, which more often than not make my stomach turn, and I wonder what kind of bastard could do that. Then I'll look at my wife looking at the photographs, lost in thought, her long brown hair trailing the table, her quick fingers tracing the shape of a corpse, and I'll think, this is my wife, who believes there are no absolutes.

"Just look," she says now, pointing at the newborn, which has somehow been transformed and is swaddled up like the baby Jesus, all clean and pink, resting in its mother's arms. While the camera was covering the lower regions, somebody thought to put orange lipstick on the mother, who now lies there, staring alternately at the baby and the camera, making kissy faces. Then the camera pans to the husband, who is also making kissy faces, and my wife looks at me as if I'd just strangled a kitten or been caught with a hooker.

Before I can defend myself from her unspoken accusation, she's crying, and to top it off she's trying to hide it. The only thing worse than my wife crying is my wife trying to pretend she isn't crying, or maybe, come to think of it, Mrs. Shevardnadze, our upstairs neighbor, leaning out her window and shouting, "I'm going to call the fire department on you!" which is exactly what she's doing right now.

Then my wife stops pretending she isn't crying, she just lets it all go, so I shut the lid on the grill and climb through the window and sit on the couch beside her and put my arms around her and say, "Baby, I'm just not ready."

"What's there to be ready for?" she says. "You and that dialectic philosophy."

She says "dialectic" like it's a dirty word, half whisper, half curse. She's good at bandying the term about, but she doesn't buy it—the connection between dialectic philosophy and my fear of procreation. She likes to say I flunked out of the Study of Either-Or, and I like to remind her that I didn't flunk out—I dropped out—and there's a big difference. One year away from a Ph.D. at what is often referred to as a venerable institution, something happened. I didn't lose interest, exactly. I didn't lose faith. I just couldn't bring myself to open another scholarly journal. When I sat down at my computer to work on my dissertation, more often than not I ended up playing solitaire, or opening the "outdated correspondence" file on my hard drive, reading old letters I wrote years ago to girlfriends whose faces I couldn't exactly remember.

"I can't do this," I said ten years ago, looking at pages and pages of small text scattered across my desk, the floor, the kitchen table. The truth was I had outdone myself. The more complex my argument became, the less I understood. I began to feel I was losing my grasp of the subject. All the threads were coming apart.

"So don't," she said.

Case closed. We got married in the Hamptons, where her parents had a place, and I became a high school teacher. My wife became, over time, a high-powered defense attorney. She gets people off the hook for crimes they may or may not have committed.

"But what if he's guilty?" I sometimes ask, standing over her at the kitchen table while she reads through stacks of legal documents. "What's guilty?" she says. "Aren't we all guilty? Is anyone really guilty? Guilt is a matter of perspective, just varying shades of gray."

Which is where we diverge whole-heartedly. I believe in black and white. Guilty or innocent. You love someone or hate her. I'm not ashamed to confess that I swallowed all that stuff hook, line, and sinker back in college—how the universe is made up of polar opposites battling against each other, how this constant conflict between good and evil, light and dark, fuels the whole world. My belief in that system never wavered, and this is at the root of my problem with babies.

A man can be either a good father or a bad one. I had a bad one. My wife had a good one. And if I were forced to choose dialectically my own fatherly potential—whether I'd be good or bad—I can't say how I'd vote. I've tried to explain that to my wife—how, until I can know with one hundred percent certainty that I would make a good father, I can't bring myself to be one. This, to me, seems fair.

"That's ridiculous," she says. "You're building a trap. You can't know until you try. But you won't try until you know. Just admit it. You don't really like kids."

"Not true," I say. "If I didn't like kids, would I be a teacher?"

She goes into the bedroom and slams the door. I can smell the steaks burning on the fire escape. Mrs. Shevardnadze is stomping around upstairs. Some kids are rapping on the street below. The M-11 rattles by. It's May, so the alley below our window smells like dog piss.

***

I teach at a prep school for boys out on the island. For years I've been lobbying the Curriculum Development Committee for a class in dialectic philosophy, but each year they refuse, labeling such modes of thinking outdated and irrelevant. So I teach American History, European Wars, and Intro to Philosophy, on top of coaching water polo, because what is more relevant in this day and fucking age than water polo? Every now and then the headmaster railroads me into moderating the chess team, even though I can't remember the last time I won a game of chess. I feel ill at ease with the other teachers, who all have advanced degrees in education—and who seem to believe that teaching is a calling, rather than an accidental vocation. My own aborted Ph.D. in philosophy feels somehow inadequate. Sometimes in the teachers' lounge the other faculty talk about pedagogical theory, or about the spiritual rewards of teaching, and I just dig into my burrito and look down at a stack of papers, pretending to prepare for class.

But one day a year, things are different. One day a year I get to teach dialectic philosophy, and that's when I really come into my own. This year, my big day happens to fall in the same week as the baby argument.

So it's the morning after the big fight, 6:30, and I'm driving to work. I want to get there early. Usually I make the trip in a zombie state, but today, I'm totally awake. I'm feeling good, really confident, thinking about how I'm going to explain dialectic philosophy to my students, how I'm going to shake them out of their indifference. Usually this drive just kills me, because Queens Boulevard goes on forever. You might as well be driving across Europe or Asia, the boulevard's so diverse. One minute you feel like you're in China, the next you're in the Middle East, at some point you hit the good old U.S. of A. The girls walking to school in their miniskirts and platform shoes look like they know a great deal more at sixteen than you'll ever know in a lifetime. Today I'm cruising through every light, one green signal after another, and I'm not even surprised, because this is the day I hit my stride, my one day a year, and you better believe the universe is working in my favor.

As I'm coming up to 42nd the green clicks over to yellow, and half a second later it's red, and I'm sitting here, slightly perturbed at this unexpected intrusion on my perfect morning, but still feeling good, because it's just one light and it'll be over with before the optimistic guy on the radio finishes predicting sunshine. It's 6:45 in the morning but the taxis are already out in full force, the newspaper stands are open, all along the boulevard people are stepping out of shops and apartment buildings with paper and briefcase in one hand, coffee in the other. It's noisy as hell, like it always is on Queens Boulevard, but today I don't so much mind the noise because it's just background music for the lecture I'm playing in my head. There are four lanes on this boulevard, all going one direction, my direction, and I'm in the fourth lane from the morgue, which is what I call this massive rectangular building made of pocked gray cement that spans the length of an entire block. The building has not a single window. The subway cars run on top of it. Where Queens Boulevard intersects 42nd, a bridge arches over the street, and below the bridge is a tunnel.

So I'm sitting at the light, and I'm watching the E train go by on my left, passing over the morgue, across the bridge, and onward. It's moving along at a pretty good pace, but I can still see the sad sleepy faces of the people going to work. And that's when I hear the screeching. You know the arc of a screech, how it begins at a high pitch, becomes even louder and higher, then somehow winds down as the moving vehicle slows, then comes to a halt. So I've got my ears tuned in and I'm listening for the wind-down, but it doesn't come; the screeching just suddenly stops, and I know something's wrong. Just then I see something coming out of the tunnel—not just anything but a Jeep, and it is literally flying, four feet off the road and wheels to the sky, and it's not headed in just any direction, it's headed straight for me.

But what is more alarming, perhaps, than the aborted screech and the upside-down flying Jeep and the horrified faces of the people on the street is the speed at which all this is happening. The Jeep isn't flying so much as it is hovering. The whole thing is happening in slow motion. The Jeep, the E train, the pedestrians on every side of me, are moving at a fraction of their regular speed, but, for some reason I cannot explain, I happen to be switched into mental fifth gear. While the rest of the world goes freeze-frame, my brain is clicking along faster than it ever has before. As the Jeep gets closer I'm planning my next move, which is to get out of my own car, which I do, and the Jeep's still coming, and it's only about six feet from me now—the Jeep drops out of the air, skids another few feet on its roof, and stops inches from my car. The wind from the falling Jeep actually blows my hair back. And I'm thinking about how I've never been prepared in my life, not once, and as I'm moving toward the Jeep, I'm wishing I could just get back in my car.

So I'm jogging over to the Jeep, sort of a fake jog because what I'd really like is for someone else to take over. But no one else is moving. In addition to the screech there was, at the moment the Jeep landed, a sickening crunch, and now everyone is looking alternately at me, and at the Jeep, and waiting for something to happen. I experience what I can only describe as a moment of clarity. For the first time in my life I have in front of me a purpose with which I cannot argue, a clear course of action.

Suddenly my nose is pressed against the back window of the Jeep, and someone is looking at me. It is a girl of about five, maybe six. This girl is hanging upside down, suspended in the Jeep's interior, her small bright body held fast in a car seat. Quite clearly she is surprised, and she is waiting for something. No, she isn't just waiting for something, she's waiting specifically for *me*, and because my mind is working at about ten times its normal speed while the rest of the world inches forward like an ice floe, I know she is waiting to be rescued. I open the door, which opens more easily than one would expect, and I say, "Don't worry, sweetheart." Very carefully I unbuckle the car seat with one hand while supporting the child with the other—I can do this because she is very light. I am struck, in fact, by how light a five-year-old girl can be—she is not much heavier than the blue-gray cat I reluctantly share with my wife. I take her out of the car and stand her upright, and she says, "Where is my lunch box? I lost my Peoples of the World lunch box." I look inside for the lunch box, wondering what this world is coming to, that a child can no longer have a simple Holly Hobby lunchbox, or a Dora the Explorer lunchbox—no, her lunchbox must be a statement about the general civility and progressiveness of her parents. A woman in the front seat—no doubt progressive, no doubt civil, but at this moment somewhat disheveled and stunned looking—turns and says to me, "Oh my God." And then, as if remembering her manners, as all well-bred persons eventually do in the face of shocking events, "Good morning."

"Hello, ma'am." I immediately regret calling her ma'am, since she's no older than I am.

The lunch box is lying on the ceiling of the Jeep within easy grasp. I pick it up and hand it to the girl. Standing there with her brown curly hair arranged quite properly and her lunch box clutched in her tiny fingers and her face a bit cross, she looks not one bit like a child who has just flown upside down in a Jeep through a tunnel and been rescued by a stranger in a stupid red baseball cap that he wears every time he teaches dialectic philosophy.

Then it occurs to me that a) my work is not done and b) having saved the child the logical next step is to save the mother and c) the rest of the world still seems stunned into inaction. I walk quickly but not too quickly—I do not want to inspire panic in the child—to the other side of the car, where the woman is hanging upside down in front of the steering wheel. Her hair is very short. I open the door. "How is my daughter," the woman says. She says it as a simple command, unquestionably authoritative, although her voice is a bit shaky.

"Your daughter is standing over there. She's all right."

She blinks once. "Okay," she says. Her eyes are extraordinarily green, so green that they cannot possibly be natural. For a moment I am nearly in love with her, but the feeling quickly passes.

"Could you please place your hands on the ceiling," I say, "like you're doing a hand stand. I don't want you to fall on your head." She does so, and I unbuckle her seat belt, being careful not to brush up against her breasts. Then I help her crawl out of the car, and she goes around to her daughter and tucks her daughter's shirt into her bright overalls, and the two of them sit down on the sidewalk.

Suddenly, the second hand moves forward, the minute hand clicks into place, and real time is restored. "Mrs. Fernandez," a boy is saying. The boy is about fourteen and he is wearing an orange vest and holding one of those signs that says *Slow Children Playing*. "Mrs. Fernandez, it's me, Jack, the crossing guard. Are you okay?"

Mrs. Fernandez looks up at Jack. "Oh," she says. "It's you. Hon, have you seen my dog?"

Just then a woman in a svelte black suit and smart heels walks up. She is one of those New York City women who could be anywhere between 29 and 45 years old and who would be wearing a svelte black suit at any hour on any day, one of those women who I am not the least bit surprised to see clutching a rather large black lab to her chest at 6:49 on a Monday morning. This woman's hair is long and perfect. It shines alluringly in what passes for sunlight on this rather dismal morning. This woman's hair is, in fact, the exact same color as the dog's coat—and it strikes me that this is a skill that only this very particular type of New York City woman has—the ability to pick up a dog that has just been tossed violently from a moving vehicle and make it look like a well-planned accessory. She walks up to Mrs. Fernandez and says, "Is this your dog, Miss? Is this black lab the dog you are looking for?"

"Oh yes, thank you."

The whole street has sprung into action now. There are suddenly a great number of pedestrians crowded around Mrs. Fernandez and her well-adjusted daughter, and they are all very concerned, and at least a dozen of them are dialing 911 on their cell phones. I walk back to my car, which is blocking an entire lane, and of course the lane is backed up and the light is green and a lot of people are honking at me. The whole thing has taken no more than three rotations of the light.

I pull away. I go to school. I give a brilliant lecture. And then, standing there in my red baseball cap, right in the middle of my brilliant lecture, I begin to doubt dialectic philosophy. I begin to sense this gray area, in which things do not have to happen one way or the other: you do not either love someone or hate her, you do not necessarily play either the hero or the fool, you are not either a great or a terrible father. A new possibility occurs to me, the possibility that, in each case, the truth lies somewhere in between. Is it possible that the accident had nothing at all to do with a parallel universe? Is it possible that, at the moment the Jeep came hovering out of the tunnel, I did not click over into some hitherto hidden world in which I behaved in a manner exactly opposite to how I would expect myself to behave? Could it be that my heroic actions on Queens Boulevard are a true representation of the man I am, and that, until now, I simply have not been tested? I have always considered myself to be a man lacking courage and conviction, but perhaps I never before encountered the appropriate situations. Is it possible that, all these years, I have insisted upon a parallel universe as a sort of crutch, a rationale for all my own weaknesses? "Yes," I say. "Here, today, I am like *this*, but in that other universe, the mirror opposite of this one, I am courageous, decisive, brilliant, witty, entertaining, compassionate, extraordinarily good-looking, and, above all, virile."

I look out at my students and sense their excitement waning, expressions of intense boredom settling across their faces. The bell rings. I am standing with chalk in hand, arm raised high, extolling a philosophy that suddenly seems flawed, when my students breathe an audible and collective sigh of relief, scramble out of their seats, and rush for the door.

I leave school immediately after the final bell. Driving home along Queens Boulevard, I scan the scene for the next debacle— hovering Jeeps, stranded motorists, dogs lost in traffic—my next golden opportunity. But the drive is uneventful. Back home, my wife is sitting at the kitchen table, the latest scene of murder spread out before her—a young victim with haunting eyes, a silver pendant dangling primly from her bruised neck. "The Pendant Murders," my wife says matter-of-factly, canvassing the photo with her magnifying glass. I step too close to the table and see a little more of the picture than I want to. The girl is blonde and thin, and her turtleneck has been cut open at the top, her throat slashed. A silver pendant dangles from her neck. The pendant is a tiny half-moon with a jewel at its center.

Beside the photos is the evening edition of the *Daily News*. My wife prefers the *Times*, makes fun of the fact that I subscribe to the sensational *Daily News*, but I have always been comforted by its simplicity, its ability to see everything in terms of black and white. The *Daily News* lacks the muddle and grind of complexity, uncertainty, weighing of the facts. I also like the visual presentation. Every day there is a huge headline over an eye-catching photo. Today, the photo reveals the blurry shape of a man in jeans and a baseball cap. His back is to the camera, and he is leaning into a Jeep, which is upside down on a busy road. Beside him on the street, looking into the camera, is a small girl in crumpled overalls. In the front seat of the Jeep there is an upside-down woman, who seems to be saying something to the man. In the photo it looks as if, having saved the child, the man is having a conversation with the mother, probably telling her not to panic, not to move her head, probably asking her appropriate questions, such as 'Can you feel your toes? Are you dizzy? Is your vision blurred?' What I know, of course, is that the man in the baseball cap is not saying anything medically sound to the woman; he is simply retrieving the child's Peoples of the World lunchbox. The headline reads, "Who Is the Hero of Queens Blvd.?"

I say to my wife, "Did you see the paper?"

"Yep. The usual stuff. Man saves mother and child from certain disaster."

"You're a cynic."

"Actually, I admire him." She puts down her magnifying glass and glances at the paper. "Cute girl," she says. Then she looks at me accusingly, the way she did when she saw the father holding the infant on *Life of Baby*, the way she does whenever a friend of hers gets pregnant.

"I'll be in the bedroom," I say.

"It's only 4:00."

"Like I said, I'll be in the bedroom."

A few minutes later, she's there, and her red summer dress is draped across the rocking chair, and she is opening the drawer of the bedside table, reaching for the condom, and I close the drawer and say, "never mind that," and her mouth is open in a slight and endearing way, and her neck is pale and convincing, and I am Parallel Lover, a new and much-sought-after super-hero—intense and nurturing, generous and rabid, strong and gentle, impeccable.

The sheets are askew. The room is hot. Down below, the phonograph man rattles by, music drifting from his cart. Mrs. Shevardnadze is screaming at her cat. The pigeons on the eaves are cooing. My wife's breathing, finally, has slowed. Her eyes are closed, her hand draped lightly over my thigh. She looks more at peace than I've ever seen her. Soon, she is asleep and smiling slightly, unaware that I am watching. In her dreams, perhaps the dead girls are receding. For a few hours, at least, she will forget the Pendant Murders; for a few hours the world will seem like a bright, inviting place. I too am willing to believe this, am willing to believe that, at this very moment, there is a tiny flame alight in the dark recesses of her womb. There, in that place so far from reach, it has already begun: a slow and certain growth, some tiny glistening thing.

SCALES

Before we met, he had passed a decade of bachelorhood in a small house in Fairhope just steps from Mobile Bay, with the aid of a trusted assistant who did his shopping, ran his errands, and occasionally shared his meals.

And then he found me. Or, it should be said, I found him. On the Fairhope Pier, on a typically moonlit night. He appeared to me first as a statuesque figure at the end of the pier, dressed in a long-sleeved shirt and linen pants. I was having a difficult time of it, having recently lost, within the span of a few weeks, a decent job and a beloved pet, not to mention a boyfriend, when I saw him standing there, so still and silent he did not seem real. I stepped off the warm sand onto the pier. When the boards creaked beneath me he turned, and only then did I understand that this splendid creature was alive.

For several moments I hesitated. Someone standing in such a way, at such a place, on such a night, surely does not want to be interrupted. Then the moonlight hit his face, and a flash of multicolored light shot off the tip of his elegant nose, and I found myself walking toward him, as the old pier wobbled and groaned.

"Stop," he called out.

It was a slightly scratchy voice, halting, as if it was out of practice.

"Why?" I called back.

"Because," was his reply.

"It's a public pier," I said.

To this, he had no answer. He turned back toward the water and took a step. For a moment I thought he might jump. But he didn't. When I reached him, he kept his back to me and muttered, "I came out here to be alone."

"Me, too. I won't bother you." Then I moved to stand beside him, and he lifted a gloved hand to shield his face.

"Please," he said.

But by then, I had already seen.

We stood for a minute or two in silence before I said the only thing I could think of to say, which was, "You're beautiful."

"I'm ghastly," he replied.

"Not to me."

He produced a small paper bag, and when he opened it I could smell hot spice and salt and the sea. It was a strong, wonderful odor particular to the Gulf Coast, and immediately I was happy to be home again, after a long time away.

"Crawfish," he said.

"I know."

I reached into the bag, took one of the hard little shells, and twisted until the tail came clean from the head. I sucked the head, something I hadn't done in years. But the juice was delicious, even more so than I remembered, tangy and sweet. The shimmering man followed suit, and it occurred to me that the boyfriend who had just kicked me out of his stylish apartment in the stylish city that had never really felt like home would never have done such a thing. I squeezed the tail end of the shell until the tender pink meat came out and popped it into my mouth. Only after I had swallowed did I have the good grace to thank him.

"No, thank you," he said. "One should never eat crawfish alone. I've been doing it far too long." The combination of the words and the way he looked at me, as if we were complicit in some dream of love, seemed to cast forward into a future when we would do this together frequently, would, in fact, do many things together. It would not be an exaggeration to say that, at that moment, I understood that the thing we were going to share would be nothing short of a life.

We sat down on the end of the pier, removed our shoes, our feet dangling in the water, and ate. He produced a couple of warm beers, which seemed to materialize from thin air. We drank them in silence. When the crawfish and the beers were gone, he began to talk. He was three years old when the scales began to appear, he explained—on his upper legs, at first. Tiny, half-moon shaped bits, hard and thin, the edges paper-sharp. Eventually the scales began to thicken and to stretch up his body—to his groin, his stomach, his arms, shoulders, neck, and, at last, his face. "The doctors could do nothing," he said.

Once he started talking, it was as if he couldn't stop. And I, who had driven away my last boyfriend with the sheer volume and excess of my words, sat and listened. For the first time in my life, I found listening to be effortless. Every now and then I'd feel a school of tiny fish moving past like a gentle wind, the mouths nibbling at my ankles.

"No one has ever loved me before," he admitted, by which I understood him to mean that no one had ever made love to him.

When he was finished, I said, "I have something to tell you."

"What is it?"

But when I opened my mouth to say it, the words would not come out. Why mar this perfect evening with my confession? I would be for him, that night, the ideal companion. I would let him think that I was the kind of woman a man might be lucky to have. You'd be a real prize, my ex had said, sliding his hands over my breasts, my hips, my thighs, if you had your mouth surgically wired shut.

"It's nothing," I said. "Never mind."

He shook the last bits of crawfish shell into the water and put the empty bottles into the paper bag. "My house is just down the beach," he said. "Do you want to come home with me?"

"Yes."

In hindsight, I understand that when he removed his glove and took my hand in his, it was meant as a silent warning. Though he held my hand as gently as he could, I could feel the scales cutting into my palm and fingers. I wondered, but did not ask, whether the affliction covered his entire body. Later that night, pressing my face into a pillow to squelch my screams, I understood that it did.

***

That first time, I was covered with lacerations. Tiny red marks all over the front of my body, like thousands of paper cuts, and also on my back where his arms had embraced me. All through the night I kept waking in pain, the fresh wounds damp with blood, my body sticking to the soft flannel sheets. Beside me, he slept soundly, his scales wet-seeming in the moonlight, his face the picture of peace. I couldn't help but feel, somehow, that I had saved him, although it would occur to me later that it was the other way around. In any event, that first morning-after, when I woke to the sound of his scaled feet clicking softly against the tile floor, I knew that I would stay with him. That I would make a home there in that house by the bay. Maybe it was the disfiguring effect of our first attempt at love—after all, I had never been loved so dramatically. More likely, it was the fact of his having accomplished something no other man had ever been able to do: with him, I had fallen easily, happily, willingly into silence.

I can say without reservation that the weeks that followed were the best weeks of my life. Days, I went out looking for a new job while he concealed himself in the house, making notes for a memoir he planned to write. He was very secretive about the book, would not let me see so much as a single page, kept the steadily growing manuscript locked away in a file cabinet. It was a house of secrets to which I was not privy, but I had my secrets too. I did not mention to him the flaw that had brought all my previous relationships, romantic and otherwise, to an abrupt and tearful end. I did not tell him that I had laid cruel waste to a long cadre of therapists, professionals who, though trained to listen, could not bear to listen to me. Or that my second-to-last boyfriend had been so put off by my incessant talking that, following our break-up, he'd taken up with a woman who rarely spoke, who made her living as a mime on the streets of New York City. I did not tell him that my own mother would not take my calls.

He had fallen in love with a certain girl, the one he met that night at the end of the pier, the one who sat silently and listened to his stories. In order to keep him, I would remain that girl. It was easier than I could have imagined: he held my rapt attention, and I, miracle of miracles, held my fevered tongue.

***

Following that first night, we went an entire month without making love, during which time my body slowly healed. Mornings and evenings, he dressed the wounds with salve. Of course, he had to wear gloves, but even so, I felt that I had never been touched so gently. Some nights, while he was sleeping, I stood in front of the bathroom mirror, peeled back the bandages, and examined my shorn skin. It was a source of fascination for me, this pain that made me feel, at the same time, horribly wounded and deeply desired.

Then, at the beginning of our second month together, I came home from work—by then I had landed a gig as a docent at the maritime museum—to find him dressed head-to-toe in a suit of clean white felt.

"Feel," he said, holding an arm out for me to touch. "It's impenetrable. I had it custom-made. The felt is the best one can buy, hand-beaten by Tuvan women in the village of Tsengal in Mongolia."

I stroked his moon-white arm. "So soft," I said. "It's beautiful."

But what I was thinking was that I missed his scales, the way they captured and reflected light, the way, when he moved across a room, he looked like a human chandelier.

Have I mentioned that his scales twinkled? Have I mentioned that, after bathing, while he stood in the middle of the tiled kitchen floor, dripping dry to avoid shredding the towels, he was like a fountain of light?

"There is a necessary flaw in the suit's design," he said, leading me to the bedroom.

"What's that?"

When we reached the bed, he turned to face me and unfastened two buttons on his groin. A flap of felt fell away to reveal that most beautiful part of him, of which I had been in awe from the beginning.

It was average in size but exceptional in appearance, covered as it was with scales of many hues, ranging from the palest white to the deepest blue. When in repose, it lay against his body like a cylindrical jewel. What cruelty, to be blessed with such a thing of beauty, but to be unable to share it with the world!

That night, separated from him by a layer of plush white felt, it was like making love to a pillow, or a human-shaped yurt. Except, of course, for the one part. Our way of making love was to be very, very still, to let the closeness of our two bodies be a substitute for motion; even so, I came away from the event cut and bleeding. Afterward, it wasn't too bad as long as I was sitting or standing still. But walking around the maritime museum, instructing eager third-graders on the mating habits of stingrays and jumbo Gulf shrimp, proved excruciatingly painful. In a way it was terrible, but in another way it made me feel as though I had happened upon an exceptional love. He was like no man I'd ever been with. I could search for years, and never find anyone like him. It was satisfying to think of the women I knew at work—the secretary with her portentous hair, or the events planner with her eternally disappointed air of someone who has just missed out on a very good party—passing through the days with their ordinary loves, while, in the little house by the bay, my own love waited, freakish and beautiful.

***

As it turned out, the suit was only an early prototype. Over the months and years it would be followed by many others, each one hand-sewn by a celebrated textile artist across the bay in Mobile, each one an improvement upon the last. An improvement in that each new suit was less obvious, more natural-looking than the one before. The white felt gave way to something thinner and somewhat flesh-colored—also smooth, but with the faint hint of human hair. He gave the textile artist photos of himself as a very young child, before the scales began to appear, and gradually, the color of the suit came to resemble, more and more, the color his skin had been prior to the affliction. That's what he called it, in his more depressive moods, when the memoir was going badly—his affliction—and I didn't have the words to tell him that it was the affliction that drew me to him, more so than his personality, which, I came to realize, was rather ordinary, or his intelligence, which tended toward the esoteric, or his humor, which could be cruel.

The suit's hair, too, became more supple and fine, placed discriminately in the appropriate places—thicker on the legs and upper arms, a lighter patch of it on the chest, and only a few stray hairs, for authenticity's sake, in the small of the back and on the wrists. By and by, the suit began to look alarmingly realistic, so one had to examine it closely to see that something was amiss, that he was wearing not his skin, but rather a suit of simulated skin, designed, ingeniously, to bruise upon impact and to emit faint odors reminiscent of the wearer's last meal. Under the proper conditions, the suit was even designed to sweat.

The suit was so realistic, in fact, that he gained a kind of confidence he'd never known before. Over time, as the suit improved to near perfection, he began to go out in public, to socialize with ordinary folk. Eventually he got a job. He kept his hair long and always wore a hat and scarf, even in the merciless humidity, in addition to a thick makeup that had been designed by a friend of the textile artist. With all of these precautions, he was able to keep his face pretty well concealed.

But at night, when he came home from his job at the finance company—something he'd dreamed of his whole life, not least of all because it smacked of normalcy and unobtrusive prosperity—he allowed me to unzip the suit and peel it off of his shimmering skin in the pastel light cast through our windows by the sleeping Gulf, and to rinse the makeup from his face, and to do the one thing I desired most, the one thing that, unbeknownst to him, kept my love for him alive: to look at him, in all his scaled and glittering glory. When he was naked, stripped of the deceptions he had so meticulously acquired in order to pass in polite society, he was nothing short of beautiful.

When it came time to make love, I willingly zipped him into the suit again. With my job, it would have been difficult to endure the all-over scarring that would have occurred if we made love without the suit. Not to mention the fact that some genetic code was at play, some peculiar aging process was afoot, so that, while his suit grew softer and more pliant with each mutation, his scales grew sharper and more pointed.

During all this time, the suit's one supposed flaw remained: one key part of his body had to remain exposed during lovemaking. According to the textile artist, it had something to do with the chemical makeup of the fabric, which could not sustain exposure to certain types of bodily fluids. So it passed that, year after year, my feminine parts bore the brunt of our lovemaking. As a result, I felt that I belonged to him, as if our union had been purified by fire: for what is love if not sacrifice?

And then, one Friday afternoon nearly a decade after that night meeting at the pier, my husband—by then, we had walked down the aisle of a non-denominational church by the sea, and feasted on champagne and crawdads while a local Zydeco band inspired the small group of wedding guests to flail about in the sand—came home to me and said, "It's been solved."

I was sitting at the kitchen table, reviewing the literature for a new live specimen the maritime museum had acquired, the *Tonicella lineate*, or lined chiton, a prehistoric-looking mollusk with a single large foot whose tongue, or radula to be precise, is covered with iron teeth. I suppose I didn't properly hear him, or didn't note the enthusiasm in his voice, because rather than asking him what exactly it was that had been solved, I was moved to share with him an interesting fact I'd just discovered in my reading. "It says here that the lined chiton can travel up to three feet on the ocean's surface to scrape algae off nearby rocks. Then it returns to its home scar, which is a depression in its own rock that is, get this, shaped just like the lined chiton." I shoved a potato chip into my mouth and kept talking. "I mean, the chiton has used his iron-coated teeth—they get that way, the teeth I mean, by a complicated chemical process called biomineralization—to shave away the rock until it fits his body just so. Like a glove! Like a lover!" I exclaimed, taking a swig of my beer, for by this point I had really made myself at home on the Gulf Coast, swigging beer and sucking crawfish heads with abandon, occasionally even attending a tent revival, forgetting that I'd ever lived in one of the strange cities of the North or that, in a past life, my logorrhea had made me intolerable.

"Says here that chitons have flexible shells," I said, "composed of eight articulating valves, which are covered with thousands of tiny eyes called aesthetes. The largest chiton in the world is the Cryptochiton stelleri, or gumboot, which can reach thirteen inches and has valves shaped like butterflies. Butterflies, mind you! Never say there isn't poetry in the sea."

My husband, at this point, was staring at me in stunned silence. And why shouldn't he? I'd never strung so many words together the entire time I'd known him. Something strange had happened that long-ago night on the pier; I had, without warning or effort, been cured. What I'd believed at the time to be a temporary reprieve from my own affliction had turned out to be permanent. Weeks turned into months, months to years, and I did not feel the need to talk. Quite the opposite, I felt compelled to silence, so that by the time I returned home each day from the museum, where it was my duty to speak at length about the wonders of the sea, I had little desire to say anything. Instead, I listened. In truth, I could not help feeling that some important part of me was missing, that I was somehow less than I had been before.

"Didn't you hear me?" my husband asked, taking a seat beside me at the table, and looking with some disgust at the oily stain the potato chips had left on my paper plate. "I said it has been solved." He was wearing Bermuda shorts, a T-shirt, and thongs—Fridays were mandatory casual day at the finance company—and his suit was so excruciatingly skin-like, so perfectly fitted to his body from neck to fingertips, that, had I not known better, I might think that he had been cured. By this point we were making love infrequently, and the intimacy we'd once shared had begun to melt away. He had taken to wearing his suit round-the-clock, even to bed, so that I rarely experienced the sweet thrill of disrobing him in the evening after work, peeling away his outer layer to reveal the man I loved.

At that moment, I felt that I was sitting across the table from someone no more familiar to me than the paperboy or the clerk at the 7-Eleven. Then, mercifully, he unwound the scarf that covered his chin, and took off his floppy hat, and brushed back his long hair, and I felt enormously grateful for this glimpse at his private self, this glimpse he allowed to no one but me.

"What's been solved?" I asked.

"This."

He stood and dropped his shorts. And there before me stood an entirely natural-looking man, adorned in curly pubic hair and dangling flaccidly in the heat, the scrotal sack appropriately wrinkled, the whole package dismally common.

"How did he do it?" I asked, reaching out to find the zipper.

At which point he began to swell at my touch, saying, "Baby, there's no zipper."

"Well then, how do we get this damn thing off?" I said, tugging at it in a completely utilitarian way, which he mistook for an erotic overture.

"There's no taking it off. I've been sealed into the suit. I can bathe in it, exercise in it, even make love in it."

By now I was using my teeth, trying to tear the wretched false skin away.

"It has to be removed once a year so that the skin can go through an aging process and any necessary alterations can be made," he panted, as if this thing I was doing with my teeth had something to do with sex, as if it were not a desperate attempt to reveal that most beautiful part of him, that most real and multi-colored thing, which was a specimen in its own right, deserving of its own field of scientific study, not to mention an entire school of experimental art and a movement in postmodern literature.

But I was no match for the suit, this soft and lifelike armor. I did not find what I was looking for.

That night, we made ordinary love. While he thrashed and thrusted above me, I faked an orgasm for the very first time. And when it was over I had nothing to say. My speech on the mighty chiton, that master of disguise who carved for itself a home in the rock and looked, to any possible predators, like nothing special, like a part of the rock itself—my speech had been a one-time thing. My logorrhea really was gone, relegated like the ex-boyfriends and the therapists and the big city to my distant past.

Before long, the textile artist came up with a way to disguise my husband's one remaining feature, his face. He fit in so well, even he seemed to forget that the skin he presented to the world was not his own. Eventually he got a promotion, and we moved across the bay to a restored antebellum home in downtown Mobile, keeping the little cottage by the bay for the sake, I suppose, of nostalgia. Mornings, I'd drive the Causeway to the maritime museum in Fairhope, watching the sun blaze over the silver bay. Afternoons, on the return trip, I'd catch a glimpse of the old warship, the U.S.S. Alabama, sitting placidly in the water, a gigantic relic of some bygone glory, its dull gray cannons barely hinting at the violence they'd once wrought upon the world.

Nights, my husband and I would sit together in our well-appointed living room, reading: he read biographies of captains of industry, while I buried myself in colorful textbooks detailing the wondrous creatures who made their home in the sea: sharpnose puffer, ocellated frogfish, mushroom scorpionfish, flying gurnard, dragon wrasse, leafy seadragon. There were pictures of sea stars and urchins, mollusks of many varieties, crustaceans of indescribable beauty.

My husband had long since given up his dream of writing a memoir. After making several attempts to break the lock of the file cabinet in which the manuscript was concealed, I finally called in a locksmith. Upon opening the drawer I saw that the book had never really been started. It was little more than a list of potential titles and chapter headings, accompanied by a few photocopied documents from the medical files of his youth. These documents were characteristically clinical in nature, but among the dull listings of medications and false diagnoses, recommended treatments and such, a little light occasionally shone through. *Upon removal of a small sample of the scales, one doctor had typed, the subject bled profusely.* Close examination of the scales under a microscope revealed a range of exceptional colors not found in nature. And then, in nearly illegible handwriting in the margin was a note the doctor had apparently scribbled to himself, an afterthought: *Rare opportunity to witness a thing of wonder. Thanked his mother profusely for bringing him to me. No diagnosis possible. Very clearly one of a kind.*

I returned the files carefully to their places and had the locksmith conceal any sign that the lock had ever been compromised. I did, however, steal from the files the one piece of paper on which the doctor had allowed himself a moment of professional awe. I keep it hidden in a secret place. Every now and then, when the ease of our ordinary lives becomes overwhelming, when I think I cannot pass another day in the shadow of my husband's brilliant disguise, I take the paper from its hiding place and review the doctor's words, and I think of the treasure I found that night on the pier in the moonlight. It is almost close enough to touch, this treasure. Sometimes I dream of some point in the future, when some ordinary disease or accident will take my husband's life, and I will lay him down in the good light of our little house by the bay, and I will go exploring. With my fingernails, my teeth, my eyes, I will search until I find his secret seam. Then I will open him up like some splendid fruit, like some creature from the depths of the mysterious sea, and behold, once again, his beauty.

HONEYMOON

She had this red hair. She liked to compare it to a pack of
rowdy schoolchildren, presentable one moment, and then all
wild and out of control the next. Her teeth were perfect and
straight, as was her back and posture. She said it was the product
of operations, braces, and odd contraptions that, with the goal
of making her ultimately attractive, had made her totally unat-
tractive at a time when those things mattered the most. High
school. If anything, she said, it had taught her at an early age
that she was going to have to work for a living. While the other
girls were meeting boys and dreaming of weddings, she was taking physics, computer science, and wood shop. Oddly enough,
it all paid off. Now, she has her own company designing kitchen
utensils. The money is in the forks and knives, she says, though
she spends most of her time on the more interesting pieces,
whisks, spatulas and rubber scrapers.

Our deal was this: she would plan the wedding, and I would arrange the honeymoon. Her only request was that it should include a stay at a nice hotel, one with turn-down service.

The wedding was remarkable, and not because the food was tremendous, the guest list artfully constructed, or the location perfectly chosen. No, the wedding was remarkable because it included me in such a prominent role. You see, I'm 39, and well, I just figured that the window had already closed on those opportunities. It's not that 39 is a horrible age. It's simply that, before I met her, I had started to feel a certain way. It felt like a movie, like I had just seen the matinee and now the reels were starting all over again for the afternoon showing. I had been having a lot of déjà vu; everything seemed to remind me of something else. Nothing was new, but rather a variation on something old. Once I met her, though, for the most part, the sense of déjà vu stopped.

First, a word about turn-down service. I can be brief because I'm sure you've probably experienced it for yourself. It's that thing you get at nice hotels, when the maid comes—usually while you're off at some meeting—and straightens things up, puts your papers together on the desk, bends down the sheets on the bed and, if you're lucky, puts a nice mint on the pillow. It's unnecessary, yes, but nice all the same.

My wife's request for a hotel with turn-down service didn't surprise me. You see, my job requires constant travel to a bunch of different countries, a bunch of different hotels. Some are good, some are bad, more often the latter.

Whenever I travel, I'll call her from the hotel, and the first question she asks is whether the place has turn-down service. She likes the idea of a bonus, something totally unnecessary but special. If I say yes, she shrieks with excitement. "Did they fold your T-shirts too?" she'll ask, and "How's the mint?" If the place doesn't have turn-down service, she'll quickly change the subject, as if she is trying to take my mind off of some bad news. It's become a joke between us. I guess it's something new to me, something I hadn't experienced before her, something I never saw in the matinee. In a way, it is this, not the beautiful hair, not the smooth skin, but rather this something else that is the very essence of what I love about her.

With that in mind, you understand how tricky it was for me to plan the honeymoon. Don't get me wrong—there are a lot of great hotels with really great turn-down services. Hotel Gellert in Budapest, the Grand Hotel in Llubjana, the Serena in Zanzibar. I've done my research. The Palace in New York probably has the best. Still, I chose the Llao Llao, a strange but amazing hotel at the foot of the Andes in Bariloche, Argentina. I studied their brochures, I browsed their website, I conferred with their concierge, and then I saved my money.

When we arrived, the manager came out and met us in person, remembering both our names and congratulating us on our wedding. He then paused for a moment, smiled, and explained that he had been able to "work some magic" (my translation), and get us a special suite on the third floor. The room has a name, which I can't pronounce, rather than a number. That's how good it is.

We arrived late, so there was no turn-down service that first night. Instead we found a bottle of champagne, along with a tasty spice cake. The next morning, we got up early and walked downstairs to the big, beautiful room where they serve breakfast. As we were walking into breakfast there was a group of people walking out. A guy, three women and a baby. The guy was my age, though tremendously good looking. He was carrying the baby, which was also tremendously good looking. The three women, possibly his wife, her mother and her sister, were unmemorable. He looked like he had been the captain of his high school football, or, I should say, futbol team. The baby was no more than a year old, but I could tell that the guy and his wife had been married a while. He had cheated on her before, I could tell right off. How did I know? I suppose it's easy, really, if you pay attention, if you watch the details.

As we were walking into the breakfast room and futbol guy and his wife were walking out, he slowed down. It was perfectly choreographed, as if he'd done it many times before. He casually gauged where his wife was, his sister-in-law, and his mother-in-law, and then he slowed a bit more. Without doing anything out of the ordinary, he was suddenly a step behind his group, out of their field of vision. He shifted his baby over to the other arm, and then he glanced over at my wife. All so measured, all so subtle. It was as if he had already planned a long-term affair with my wife, and now he was simply being careful to conceal the evidence.

"It looks like you're going to the prom," I said to my wife.

"With futbol guy?" she said, smiling. "Really?"

"Yep."

Later that night, we were in our room, still marveling at the view. We were preparing to go down to the hotel restaurant for dinner, when there was a knock on the door. I pulled on my pants and went to answer. It was the housekeeper. She said something in Spanish, something that I probably could've translated from ten different languages. I turned to my wife, "She wants to know if we would like turn-down service."

"Turn-down service!"

My wife squealed with joy, jumping up and down. Literally, she was jumping up and down—that's how happy she was. Nobody jumps up and down, but she was. It was terrific.

Just then, in the hallway, behind the maid, futbol guy's mother-in-law walked by, holding the baby. Then his sister. Then his wife. Then him. With everyone out of range, he quickly glanced past the maid and into our room, past me, and to my wife. She was barely dressed, her hair wildly out of control, her nails still painted white from our wedding, her hands in the air, jumping up and down, totally beautiful.

All in a second.

And in a second, I had my first full déjà vu since I had met her. Okay, maybe it wasn't a déjà vu, but it was a very clear and unavoidable memory.

Years earlier, I had had a different job with a smaller company. We were nearly bankrupt, and things were looking bad. My boss, the owner, felt that if we could just finish this deal we'd been working on, it would save the company and everyone's job. We had a receptionist and two accounting clerks who were depending on us. The deal involved this slightly eccentric older guy. Everyone else was ready to agree, but he had final approval. Unfortunately, it was June, and he had just returned to his homeland for the entire summer. It was his wish that he spend one last summer at his family's old cabin in this remote rural village. The problem was three-fold: his homeland was far away, there was a war going on, and the village had no phone service. Idiotically, I volunteered to go see the guy in person.

About the country: it was a beautiful place with a discouraging, endless war. As far as I could tell, the war was between a bunch of people who all looked pretty much the same, killing each other for being so different. The war had been going on for two years, and most of the fighting took place in the new capital. You probably saw it on television. All of the tall buildings were destroyed, windows broken, concrete missing. Snipers were hidden in every nook and cranny. The main street, the Boulevard of Heroes, was littered from one end to the other with old cars and dead drivers, all the product of one or two small bullet holes. The snipers were so prevalent and determined, that if someone was shot in the middle of the Boulevard, they would have to die where they lay because no one could risk running out to get them. Needless to say the place was a ghost town.

The eccentric guy did not live in the new and dangerous capital, but rather in a small village only six kilometers away. Through copious research, I learned that, after two years, the Ministry of Transportation was going to resume bus service to the new capital. It was a symbolic thing, a desperate attempt to reestablish some semblance of normalcy. The Ministry didn't actually think anyone would take the bus anywhere near the brutally violent city. When I, an American, showed up on that first morning, asking for a ticket to the town just barely west of the new capital, the ticket agent was stunned. She tried to talk me out of it, but I had no other form of transportation.

When we left the first station, there were six people on board, including the driver. By stop number four of ten, it was just the driver and me. He was very fidgety, nervous but oddly jovial. I tried to speak with him, but our languages had not a single word or gesture in common. He was wearing a bulletproof vest and chain-drinking liter bottles of beer. It took hours to cross the rough terrain. Every now and then a road would be out, and we would have to take a detour. I sensed he was making the detours up as he went, winding in the general direction of the capital, hoping I'd change my mind. Around three in the morning, it began to snow. I had been traveling for 38 straight hours, if you count the taxi ride to the San Francisco airport. I was very sleepy, utterly exhausted. I was starving and thirsty. I hadn't even brought a coat. The windows iced over, and I was freezing.

Although the driver had turned up the stereo loud, some pan-flute folk music with a surprisingly catchy chorus, I still was having tremendous trouble fighting the urge to sleep. And that was the problem: if I fell asleep, I would miss my stop, stop number nine. Stop number ten, the final stop, was at the wrong end of the Boulevard of Heroes. Past the littered cars and bodies, past all of the determined snipers.

And that's it. That's the memory, the déjà vu, whatever. Standing there in the doorway to our beautiful suite in the luxurious Llao Llao Hotel, caught between the futbol hero and my wife, all I could remember was a late night on a freezing bus, snow coming down, sleep almost irresistible, rocking back and forth in my uncomfortable seat, repeating to myself over and over, "Don't fall asleep, don't fall asleep, don't fall asleep, don't fall asleep."

HOSPITALITY

My wife and I had just left the party and were driving across the Bay Bridge toward the Oakland Hills. Or rather she was driving, because she was in control and wanted me to know it, wanted to be certain I harbored no illusions about my own potency or free will. "Look buddy," she was saying, without so much as opening her mouth or looking my way, "our Friday afternoon and our general direction, our speed and velocity, indeed, our very lives, are at my discretion, no need for input from you, thank you very much."

My wife was staring straight ahead, gripping the steering wheel at ten and two. At the party, which was held in the faculty lounge of the community college where I serve as Dean of Administrative Affairs, my wife had been treated viciously, as she often is at these gigs, because my colleagues do not appreciate her role as a high-powered defense attorney, and they were in an uproar over her latest case. The victim was a fifty-four-year-old politician who had shady dealings involving the new airport, but despite this he was much beloved by educators because he built a city park and was a big supporter of city funding for the college. He was found two weeks ago in the stairwell at the Civic Center with three stab wounds to his neck. My wife is representing the suspect.

Half an hour into the party I found her near the exit, surrounded by a theology professor, an English adjunct, and a guidance counselor, my wife's only defense a Chinette plate which she held aloft, the food untouched: a miniature sausage wrapped in a Pillsbury biscuit, a Wheat Thin topped with Cheez Whiz, and four pretzel sticks.

"How could you defend that monster?" the guidance counselor asked, tugging at my wife's sleeve. "Really," said English adjunct, "isn't it open and shut?" The theology professor, who used to be the pastor of a Southern Baptist church that was in the papers some years ago over a scandal involving a group of teenaged evangelicals, just stood there silently, staring at my wife's earlobes, about which he had once remarked, inappropriately I thought, "Your wife has the most delicate ears."

She looked to me for salvation.

"Hon?" I asked, prepared to assume the role of rescuer, chivalrous knight, defender of defense attorneys. I stepped into the circle and made a subtle indication with my watch.

With a look of relief, she said to the gang of aggressive pedagogues, "We have to be going." She was wearing a dark blue suit in which she looked very good, very sexy, even though that was not her intent. Her hair was pulled back and twisted at the nape of her neck with a little velvet contraption I'd acquired by calling a 1-800 number. It was called the Hairdini, and it came with an instructional video. With this device my wife was able to contort her hair into serpentine shapes that suggested mystery and warmth and intense sexual energy, all of which she has, although I would never say that to her, because saying it would be a breech of etiquette, for reasons that I can't quite explain.

Something in my wife's tone was so forceful that the three inquisitors parted when she spoke. As she moved away from them I saw a row of New Yorker cartoons descending the wall where she had been standing, each framed in black construction paper, and I suddenly felt ashamed of this institution that had become my life, the predictable humor and petty battles that played out daily in this bastion of lesser academia.

My wife took the cracker smeared with Cheez Whiz, pressed it past her very red lips, and tossed the Chinette plate into a trash can. She chewed meticulously, staring at me. I felt a soft and unsettling erection, and I imagined she was swallowing me up, imagined I was dying in the embrace of her magnificent teeth, and I thought of the lines from a Brautigan poem—"the beautiful woman that became my wife, the mother of my children and the end of my life"—only in the poem, of course, the wife is at home making dinner for Brautigan's friends, and my own wife would never do such a thing.

Outside, we snaked our way through the parking lot, past Jeep Grand Sports, the dusty Volvo station wagons, and Andy Sartello's Harley, which my wife looked at, I am convinced, in a wistful manner. Approaching the luxurious green sports car, a gift from one of her clients, my wife said in that controlled voice of hers that parts crowds and convinces juries and calms the most virulent defendants, "I'll drive."

"Where are we going?" I asked.

"Oakland."

"How long will this take?"

"Thirty minutes. Maybe an hour. Jolina isn't expecting us."

"Jolina?"

"Frank's wife."

"Why do we need to see her?"

"She's Frank's alibi," my wife said. "I have to ask her what he was doing on the night of you-know-what."

Frank was my wife's client, the guy who'd stabbed the politician on the stairwell at the Civic Center. The last thing I wanted to do was listen to Frank's wife explain why her husband couldn't possibly have killed the politician. But earlier that day, as my wife and I were getting ready for the party, she said, "Afterwards, we'll drop by and see this woman I need to see," and I said, "Okay," because everything between us is a give and take, a contract borne out in silent agreement and unspoken animosity, though that is not to say we are not both gracious in our compliance with the terms of the contract. Marriage, I have found, is a kind of lifelong hospitality, a polite observance of protocol executed daily and with a good measure of deceit.

Traffic was thick and the bridge seemed to go on forever. Out the window I could see the bay, steely and bleak in the fog, and up ahead the shining gray triangles of the bridge, connecting and parting, dissecting the sky, a complex industrial geometry that never fails to make my head swim, and beyond the bridge the shipping towers, huge and almost Orwellian in the mist. Then we were driving up Grand, past the Grand Lake Theater, and every light was yielding to my wife, who was so sure of her timing that she didn't even bother to slow down when she approached a red light, she just kept barreling forward, and each light miraculously turned green just as she was about to break the law. What killed me, I mean what really killed me, was the fact that she didn't even seem to notice the whole goddamn machinery of the planet was wired in her favor.

I said, "So did he do it?" and she said, "Who?" and I said, "Frank," and she said, "Of course not," and I said, "What about the blood on his boots? What about the DNA? What about his fingerprints?" and she said, "That's all circumstantial."

We pulled onto a cul-de-sac, something out of the fifties with perfect lawns and blonde children on bikes. My wife looked in the rearview mirror and smoothed her already smooth hair. "This is it," she said. The house was very clean and new. I was feeling nervous, but excited; as far as I knew, I'd never been in a murderer's house before. As we walked up the sidewalk, edged with ice plants thrusting their spikes toward the sky, I imagined Jolina opening the door. She would be dressed in a silk kimono, wearing suggestive heels with straps barely wide enough to keep her toes in, and she'd be sporting plenty of jewelry and make-up, some real strong perfume, and she'd be talking on the phone with one of her shady lovers, who was telling her what a time they'd have, just the two of them, now that old Frank was in jail. She would want me badly, and I would want her, too, the sexual energy between us in the room would be a thing to contend with, but we would communicate to one another with subtle and meaningful glances that it was not meant to be.

My wife rang the doorbell and adjusted my tie and said, "Be polite."

The door opened. An average-looking woman stood before us, wearing a pair of jeans, a pressed white shirt, and sensible black boots. "I wasn't expecting you," she said.

"I just wanted to chat with you about Frank," my wife said. Chat. She's something. "This is my husband," she added, an afterthought. "We were out and about, so I invited him to join me."

Jolina smiled. "Come in."

We passed through a long hallway into the living room. There were a couple of framed prints of flowers on the walls, like the ones you get from Ethan Allen, the kind of art that's designed to match the furniture while revealing nothing about the owners. Everything was neat and tasteful, with the exception of a plaster statuette of two lovers embracing in a rather acrobatic way. "Have a seat," Jolina said. "Would you like something to drink?"

My wife pinched my elbow, by which she meant that I was not to have a drink. I almost said no thank you, but then I thought, I am a grown man. It is Friday afternoon and I am a responsible person, the Dean of Administrative Affairs at the top-ranked community college in the northern part of the state, no less, and, unlike my wife, I am not under any professional obligation to this woman, and the appropriate thing to do in this situation is to have a drink. It even occurred to me that if I turned down the drink Jolina might think I was a recovering alcoholic, and I didn't want to give her that impression, so I said, "Why yes, thank you."

"What will you have?"

I tried to sound casual, as if I was not here with the defense attorney, who held Jolina's husband's life in her hands. "What are my choices?"

Jolina glanced over her shoulder toward the kitchen, as if she shared with it some unspoken communion, as if it held the key to mysteries as yet unconsidered by the majority of the human race. "Gin, bourbon, vodka, Scotch—blended and single-malt—and, of course, all the necessary mixers," she said, her green eyes bright with possibility. "Wine, white or red. In the beer department, I have Anchor Steam, Amstel Light, Miller Genuine Draft, Guinness, and Grolsch. Oh, and if it's too early for that, I have the usual: Calistoga, Coke, Diet Coke, Dr. Pepper, Sprite, milk, an assortment of Mexican soda, a variety of fruit juices."

I was impressed. Here we were, unexpected guests on a Friday afternoon, and this woman had every right to be nervous, downright frantic. Instead, she played the perfect hostess. Not only was she in full possession of her wits, but she also had every possible drink to offer. I must admit I was humbled in her presence. I remembered the first party my wife and I ever threw as a married couple. Back then, we were what might be classified as "the intellectual poor," and we'd spent far more than we could afford on an assortment of liquor and some fancy swizzle sticks. Half an hour into the party we ran out of mixers, and there was a great commotion over who would go where to purchase all the necessities we'd forgotten. By the time my friend Bob came back with tonic and orange juice, crushed ice and Coke, bev-naps and sugared almonds and pistachios and chips, the guests were disgruntled and forlorn and moving toward the door. The party could not be salvaged. We haven't thrown one since. I've begun to suspect that a person's value as a human being is directly proportionate to his or her ability to host a party.

"What will it be then?" Jolina was saying, with that air of firm, no-nonsense patience that all good hosts possess.

"Gin and tonic," I said, immediately regretting my choice, which, though refreshing, might be taken as a sign of weakness. I should have asked for Scotch.

"Will Tanqueray Ten be all right?"

"Perfect."

I could go on about the exquisite geometry of the three cubes of ice stacked in the small square glass, which shone slightly blue under the pleasing skylight and fit perfectly in my hand. Or about the pleasing quinine tinge of the tonic blended so expertly with the Tanqueray Ten, or the plate of miniature spinach quiches and the fragrant cheese board Jolina set before us—as if she kept such things around the house in case of unexpected guests—or about the cool Art Deco music emanating from invisible speakers, or the way she made me feel so at ease as I sat there on her plush white sofa—more at ease, in fact, than I felt in my own home. But that is really beside the point. After all, we were there for her alibi.

My wife talked to Jolina about area schools, about the supermarket down the street that was being remodeled, and about Spreckels Lake in Golden Gate Park, which they had both frequented as children. Finally my wife got around to asking about Frank, a question which she slipped so seamlessly into the conversation I almost missed it.

"Oh, I remember that night very clearly," Jolina said, leaning forward. "Frank was helping me paint the upstairs room—it took hours. We're expecting, you know."

"Congratulations!" my wife and I said simultaneously.

Oh, Lord, help me, is what I was thinking. If there's anything sexier than a pregnant woman who hasn't yet started to show, I don't know what it is. I wondered if Jolina could tell I was turned on. I crossed my legs and took a long gulp of my drink; I could sure use another.

"Would you like to see the nursery?" Jolina offered.

"Of course." We followed her upstairs, where she opened a door onto a yellow room. All the windows were open and an electric fan was turned up high, its wired white face rotating slowly back and forth. The breeze caught me in the face, filling my nose with the faint scent of paint.

"We wanted to go with a neutral color," Jolina said. "We've decided not to know the gender ahead of time.

I considered telling her something I'd read in *House Beautiful*, that most family fights occur in the kitchen because so many kitchens are yellow, a color that causes anger and aggression. I considered telling her in great detail about the fight my wife and I had had the previous week in our very own yellow kitchen, when she demanded to know exactly how many drinks I'd had that month and then bandied about insulting phrases like "lingering immaturity" and "inadequate long-term goals." I considered telling Jolina about the children's book I'd written, which honest-to-God was being published by a New York publisher, and about how it was the realization of a life-long dream. But Jolina was so happy about the nice color of the baby's room, I didn't mention it. I decided I'd send her a copy of the book when it came out. While reading *The Enchanted Chimney*, savoring the delicate slant rhymes and laughing at the subtle double entendres meant to amuse clever parents, Jolina would think of me, would remember how good I looked on her sofa, my elegant hands wrapped around the blue glass. She would probably read the book several times a day for a week, before finally working up the nerve to call and ask me over for cocktails.

"It looks lovely," my wife said.

"Thank you. The crib will go over there."

Jolina shut the door and we went back downstairs. Something in me applauded her determination to lie for her husband. I wondered if my own wife, given similar circumstances, would lie for me. Had she noticed the faint smell of paint? Years ago, when she was still in law school and we were barely making it on my adjunct pay, I took odd jobs painting. A newly painted wall has a certain sheen that lasts two, three days at most. The yellow room had that sheen. It couldn't possibly have been painted two weeks before, which meant Frank wasn't helping Jolina paint the room on the day of the murder. His alibi was bogus.

Back in the living room, Jolina showed us a care package she was putting together for Frank. In it was a pair of socks she had knitted, some books, and a few photographs of the two of them in happy poses—walking on Ocean Beach, hiking at Point Reyes, holding hands and kissing in front of the chapel at The Presidio—Jolina in a pale blue dress, Frank looking handsome and law-abiding in a three-button black suit. "And I'm going to make him chocolate chip cookies," Jolina said. "He loves those." I was touched by her ability to believe in her husband's innocence, even as she lied for him. I wondered if my wife would be able to muster such irrational faith in me.

We talked until the kitchen clock said 6:25. As we were standing to leave, Jolina reached up and tucked her hair behind her ear, and I noticed a spot of yellow paint on the pale curve of her neck. I wanted to kiss that spot of paint, I wanted to make love to her, I wanted to be her guest forever and always, to sit in the plush depths of her sofa and accept sparkling drinks from her steady hands. I could do so much for her, I could be her man on the outside, the reliable one, the one who'd never do her wrong. Instead I took my glass to the sink and rinsed it, while she protested mildly from the living room. I ran my fingers over the cool marble countertops, breathed in the scent of dish soap and something else—lavender, maybe? Citrus? For a moment I pretended I lived in that warm welcoming house with Jolina, that she took good care of me and treated me with kindness, like a fifties housewife.

Jolina walked us out to the car, shook our hands, and said to my wife, "Frank would never hurt anyone, you know. I hope you can bring him home."

"Don't worry," my wife said, but I could hear the undercurrent in her voice, a touch of uncertainty no doubt inspired by this new and accidental revelation, the matter of the paint.

I wanted to offer my own reassurance, to tell Jolina she'd thrown the best party I'd been to in quite some time, that her child would be intelligent and brave, that I knew she'd do just fine with or without Frank. Instead I said, "It was nice to meet you."

For several minutes my wife and I drove in silence. On Grand Avenue, I turned to her and said, "Would you do that? If I committed a crime, would you lie for me?"

"Why do you ask?" she said. And then, to deflect the question, "Would you?"

"Yes."

"There's your answer."

It was quiet in the car as we cruised down Grand Avenue, all the lights synchronized in her favor. I had married such a capable woman, I sometimes felt afraid.

"Would your lie be better than Jolina's?" she asked.

"I like to think so," I said, silently willing Jolina to get it right, to improve her execution of their chosen alibi. I thought of her and Frank in the yellow room with the new baby. I imagined their clean and meaningful life, the lemon cake and rich coffee she would offer to members of the PTA when they came to visit, the fine parties she would host for the child's birthdays and graduations.

"If I did go to prison," I said, "would you make me a care package?"

"Sure."

"What would you put in it?" I pressed, imagining our new life of small kindnesses and daily hospitality, her heart warmed by my desperate plight.

"Chocolate chip cookies."

"Homemade?"

"Of course."

"But you've never made me chocolate chip cookies before," I said.

"You've never needed them."

"How do you know that?"

We were approaching the toll booth, and the cars were beginning to bottleneck.

People were honking and giving each other dirty looks. My wife swerved expertly to avoid a blue Honda Civic that cut in front of us, then reached up and with one swift motion unhooked the velvet contraption in her hair. Her long dark curls uncoiled. "Trust me," she said, somehow managing to give me a seductive and almost loving look while navigating the traffic. "I know."

The fog had shifted, so that it formed a wide, fast-moving circle around the city. The Bay Bridge stretched out beneath a perfectly blue swath of sky. I reached for my wallet, preparing to retrieve the toll, when my wife began to navigate the complex matrix of fast-moving lanes, first one, then another, and another, a space magically opening for her each time, until we were cruising along in the smoothest lane, the one labeled Fas-Trak, and my wife did not so much drive through the gate as she glided through it, while behind us, in the rearview mirror, I watched the chaos of other cars left behind and struggling, the towers of Oakland's shipyards disappearing in the fog.

LOVE

He doesn't want to say that his wife has changed. But she has. Something essential in her has been altered. When he met her she was soft and joyful, and she wore her relative poverty like a badge of honor. She shopped at thrift stores and ate ice cream. Stayed up late working. God, she was ambitious. There was so much she wanted from life, so much she demanded of herself.

Now her desires, her demands, have shifted outward. She runs her household like a corporation. She wants her children to be smarter, more competitive, so she packs their afternoons and weekends with language classes and music lessons and organized sports. She wants her husband to be more attentive, so she fills their calendar with date nights and weekend getaways, outings with other couples to restaurants with extensive wine lists. When was the last time they bought sandwiches at a deli and ate them on the beach?

She wants a different kitchen; she spends hundreds of hours choosing fixtures, paint, marble countertops. Those wasted hours, he thinks. Those wasted conversations.

Her body is a rock. She's taken up running and resistance training, pilates on Tuesdays, Cross Fit on Thursdays. She is in the best shape of her life. "Men no longer look at me," she complains. "You get older, and women still look."

"It's not about age," he tells her.

"Then what is it about?"

"You're beautiful," he says, trying to change the subject. In fact, she is only forty. He looks at women her age, and older, all the time. How to tell her that her body, so muscled, so disciplined, so hard and angular, is like a stop sign? When he holds her, his hands press into bone and muscle. He used to love the pillowy feel of her hips, the slight cushion of her belly. He's heard her boasting to friends that she's down four sizes from their wedding. She's so lean that her body looks stingy. When they go out to dinner, she invariably demands some variation to the dish. She orders fish but wants it grilled, with no butter. She refuses the bread, the dessert. She stares angrily at his potatoes.

"It's this town," he says to her. "We should move."

"What's wrong with the town?"

What's wrong with the town is what is wrong with her. She used to love to drive to the beach on the edge of the city, with its graffiti-spattered seawall and sand dunes covered with ice plant. Now, when she says "beach," she means Hawaii. She used to love easy weekends, reading the paper and going to the movies. Now, they spend winter Fridays driving to their rented cabin in Tahoe, wrestling with snow chains. The children, pale from exhaustion, beg to quit ski team, but she already dropped a few thousand on equipment. "It's crazy that we don't own a place up there," she says.

Crazy. He remembers their first vacation. They took a driving trip in his old Nissan Stanza, through Texas and Alabama, down to the Florida panhandle. They slept in shabby motels and ate at Denny's. They made love everywhere they went. She was beautiful and a little sloppy. She bought a sundress from the Daughters of the American Revolution charity shop in Galveston and wore it for a week with a pair of old cowboy boots she'd had since high school. She gained a few pounds from all the milkshakes and hash browns and didn't care. She loved to kiss him, couldn't get enough of him. She wanted sex anywhere and everywhere. She'd make him pull off on the side of the road to do it. She was kind to everyone. She left big tips she couldn't afford. She got excited about roadside attractions. His best friend described her as sweet. God, she was sweet.

When he hears her berating the housekeeper, his heart breaks.

He can't say, "I don't recognize you."

Instead he says, "If you expected from yourself one tenth of what you expect from others."

This ends badly. There are tears and recriminations. She takes a weekend getaway, saying she needs time to herself. She actually uses the phrase retail therapy. He feels sick. What has happened to her, to them? If he had been less successful, if she had been required to work, if they had not chained themselves to this monstrous house in this ridiculous town, would she still be the woman he once knew?

When she returns, he apologizes, even though he doesn't believe he has done anything to apologize for. Still, he wants to make things right. He wants her back, the woman he fell in love with, the woman who fell in love with him.

"This town is toxic," he says, "Let's go somewhere else. We can downsize. We can all spend more time together. We can rent a cottage on the Gulf Coast. The kids can play in the surf and hunt sand crabs. You can work again, if you want."

For a moment, she softens. He feels a glimmer of hope. He is waiting: for the sign that she still loves him, that she still loves their children, that she is capable of love at all.

TRAVEL

We first spotted them at Gate B27 in Dallas International Airport. Both were tall, blonde, and neatly dressed. I got the feeling their physical similarities brought them together, two people looking for near copies of themselves, albeit in the opposite sex. She stared at me while he was engrossed by his book, a paperback with embossed gold lettering on the cover. The title of the book was *All of Us*.

The woman stared a second too long. I hid behind *The Dallas Morning News*. "Is she still looking?"

"Yes," Jim said.

"What does she want?"

"Maybe she knows you."

"I've never seen her before in my life."

On the plane, the blonde couple sat right behind us, so close I could smell the light, flowery scent of her perfume. Every now and then I'd peek through the crack between our seats and they'd be whispering to each other. When they caught me spying they'd stop talking.

Finally we descended toward the runway in San José del Cabo. To the left I could see the desert mountains, sanded a dull brown, and to the right the lush sea, blue and roiling. It was early evening, and a yellow light shimmered over the mountains, the sea, the tip of the airplane's wing. We stepped off the plane into a dry pleasant stillness. After passing through customs, where a crumpled man gave our passports a cursory glance, Jim and I followed a driver named Lupe to an old blue van and climbed in. Minutes later the couple boarded the van and sat behind us.

"Surprise," I whispered. We looked straight ahead, but the man leaned forward and said in an unnaturally loud voice, "Hello. We're the Thompsons. How often do you do this?"

I turned around and got my first good look at him. His face was pleasant and eager, his hair wavy; he looked like one of those guys you see modeling off-brand slacks in the Mervyn's catalog. His wife was a few years his senior and was holding a big orange beach bag on her lap. On top of the bag was a brochure for their hotel: *Westin Regina. No Barriers.* The front of the brochure had pictures of surgically proportioned women in small bikinis frolicking in the surf.

"It's our first time to Mexico," I said, vaguely sensing that I wasn't answering the appropriate question, that by *this* he meant something other than vacations to Mexico, although I wasn't sure. "What about you?"

"This is our second year," she said. "Our first to Mexico, but our second time to do this. Last time it was Puerto Rico."

"We live in Chicago," the man said. "I have psoriasis, and the salt air and heat is good for my condition." He held up his arm and showed us a large brown patch stretching from elbow to wrist.

The woman shifted in her seat and looked down at the floor, and he glanced over at her, apologetic-like, and reached for her hand but she wouldn't take it. I got the feeling he was always making inappropriate comments that turned people off to them as a couple, always confessing things best saved for later. I got the feeling maybe she couldn't forgive him for doing this, but it was a habit he couldn't break, born of desperation and a naive kind of honesty.

"Oh," I said. "My dad had that." It wasn't true, but I wanted Mr. Thompson to know I didn't hold the psoriasis against him.

"Really?" Mr. Thompson said.

And then I realized "had" was probably the wrong word choice, as it implied that my dad might have died from psoriasis, so I added, "He died of liver cancer." Also untrue. I added a few small details to make the lie more credible: "Last month. He was 93. The funeral was in New Orleans."

There was another awkward pause. Mrs. Thompson said, "I'm sorry to hear that," and Jim said, "It's okay. They weren't close." I marveled at his ability to take a white lie to its logical end, to twist the lie in such a way as to make everyone feel as comfortable as possible.

I stared out the window. Small motels rose up between stretches of unoccupied beach and desert brush. Skinny cacti lined the median. The roadside was crowded with dilapidated billboards advertising perfume and cigarettes, health clubs and tequila. Finally a grand resort came into view, all red and blue stucco lit up against the cool brown evening. Lupe pulled into the long driveway winding down toward the beach. The resort was called Westin Regina. Attractive Mexican youth in hotel uniforms were standing around in the open lobby. The lobby was just a pale elegant slab of marble nestled under some rustling palm trees, no walls or windows. No barriers, as Mrs. Thompson's brochure promised.

The couple got out of the van. "Have fun," I said.

Mr. Thompson looked confused. "Oh, you're not staying here?"

"We're at Solmar."

"We'll be here for a week," Mrs. Thompson said. "Call us. We'll get dinner, drinks, see how it goes."

"Okay, we'll do that," I said, knowing that we wouldn't. They seemed too desperate somehow, too needy. I could imagine them hanging onto us through the whole vacation, sapping our attention, grinding on our nerves. I thought about a girl I knew in grammar school named Doris, who wore fuzzy yarn ribbons in her hair and followed me earnestly from first to fifth grade, each year inviting me to a birthday party at which I was the only guest.

In our room that night, with the sea breeze coming in from the balcony and the sound of fireworks thundering in the distance, we leafed through the complimentary Cabo magazine. On page 57 there was an ad for the Westin Regina. "They have passion," the ad said. "They have fun. They have…*no barriers*." At the bottom of the page, in big yellow letters: "Westin Regina. Where The Lifestyle meets the sun. Choose your travel partner wisely."

"Why do you think they capitalized The Lifestyle?" I said. "Is that code for something?"

"Swinging," Jim said. "Wife-swapping. You take mine, I'll take yours." He was concentrating on the ad, reading the fine print.

I thought of Mrs. Thompson's parting words—we'll *see how it goes*. "Oh my God. Do you think the Thompsons—"

"Yep."

"Do you think they think we do too?"

"Looks that way."

Jim was in the best mood he'd been in since we left home. I imagined breasts, hands, hairy chests, a spidery tangle of arms and legs. Suddenly I felt nervous. I yanked the magazine out of his hands. "So how did you know what The Lifestyle means, anyway?"

"I had this second cousin from Wisconsin. He was involved with that stuff."

"How come you never mentioned it before?"

"I hardly know the guy. He told me about it several years ago at a family reunion. He was drinking bourbon and Coke and he was depressed and all, and it just slipped. What happened was, I said to Walt, 'Sorry to hear about the divorce,' and he said 'I can't blame Darlene. I have to blame The Lifestyle.' Then he tells me how they used to go down to Boca Raton three times a year to partake. He said it was like some kind of smorgasbord. One minute you have a slab of Wisconsin cheddar in front of you, and the next minute, you're in The Lifestyle, and whoa, there's this platter with the Wisconsin cheddar, plus the double crème brie, the havarti, the camembert, the smoked gouda, the works. And suddenly the double crème brie looks better than the Wisconsin cheddar. Walt, see, he's this pale, overweight guy, and he was the cheddar."

"That's how he put it?"

"Maybe he was the Velveeta. That's not the point. Point is Darlene suddenly saw what life was like with the full cheese board."

I was thinking about Jim's pale, fat second cousin Walt taking his skinny little wife to Boca Raton, and how there'd be all those tan men down there in their plaid shorts, with their muscled legs, their deck shoes, and how Walt must have regretted ever getting Darlene involved in all that.

"Poor Walt didn't stand a chance," I said, putting my arms around Jim's neck. The talk of broken marriages had made me feel affectionate. "Do you want to make love?"

"Not yet."

"Does that mean maybe later?"

"Of course."

In the old days, if I wanted sex all I had to do was unsnap my bra or pat Jim in a certain way in the small of the back or give him this, "Hey, I'm your wife" look from across the room, but lately there always had to be conversation, negotiation, deliberation. I couldn't figure out when or why sex had lost its spontaneity, becoming some official act demanding diplomacy.

"Okay," I said. "What should we do, then?"

"Let's check out the beach."

A light breeze was blowing, and the white hotel rising against the bleached rock in the moonlight reminded me of some place I'd been as a child. The beach was deserted except for an elderly woman in a red swimsuit doing leg lifts on her towel. We asked her to take our picture, which she did, but then she insisted on taking the same picture several times. "Your eyes were closed," she said the first time, then, "I cut your heads off," then, to me, "Hon, suck your stomach in."

After returning to our room and showering we lay naked in bed watching a sexy show. The show was in Spanish and I couldn't understand the words, but I could tell that the characters on the show lived lives of wild abandon, of great passion and sexual urgency. I started rubbing Jim's back. "Seriously," I said. "Would you ever?"

"Ever what?"

"You know. Like the Thompsons."

"It would have to be the right couple," he said.

I traced the spatter of light brown moles on his back. "How would you know when you found the right couple?"

"They'd be about our age," he said, "and good-looking, of course." He rolled over and looked at me. "Like the Thompsons. Maybe we should call them."

"You're kidding, right?"

"Maybe."

That night I dreamt of a famous young Hollywood couple. In the dream, they were sitting in our suite, wearing terrycloth robes. The man, dark-haired and tan, started kissing me. The woman, red-headed and softly lit, offered my husband a drink. She had very pale and lovely feet. She slid her foot up my husband's leg, and then I woke. I couldn't go back to sleep after that. I felt sad and vaguely frightened.

***

The next few days we lounged on the beach, went snorkeling at the Santa Maria coral reef, and watched whales breaching as they journeyed, slow and slick-backed, from the Sea of Cortez into the wide cold Pacific. We drank a great deal of Tecate and margaritas, ate fried eggs with tomatoes and peppers, lobster tail and shrimp with molé sauce, thick tortilla chips dipped in guacamole. By the time we got back to our room each night we were too tired and hot and full for sex.

On our final evening, nursing sunburns and a vague sense of malaise, we walked into town for dinner. We chose a little restaurant a few blocks from the beach, a thatch-roofed hut run by a man from Croatia. The restaurant was crowded with locals and tourists. A mariachi band was playing by the bar. We took the only available table, which was on the outdoor patio and close enough to the road that we could smell exhaust from passing cars. We had just ordered our drinks when my husband spotted the Thompsons down the sidewalk, walking in our direction.

"Should we invite them to dinner?" Jim asked.

We'd been in Cabo for five days, with only each other for company. By then we'd grown slightly argumentative and bored. "If you really want to," I said.

Jim got up and disappeared into the sidewalk crowd. In a couple of minutes he was back, the Thompsons by his side. Their faces were slightly burnt. She was wearing a strapless white top, and bathing suit lines cut across her shoulders.

"Hello," they said in unison.

"Hi. I never got your first names."

"Steve," he said. "This is Rebecca."

The waiter appeared with two more menus, and we ordered a pitcher of margaritas and the seafood sample appetizer. We talked about snorkeling and deep sea fishing, about movies and antique gramophones, the latter of which the Thompsons collected, about UPS versus FedEx. We were having ourselves a regular conversation until, three pitchers into the evening, Jim looked up from his chile relleno and said to Steve, "So tell us about the wife-swapping."

Rebecca looked at him as if he'd just spat in the communion cup. "It's no longer called wife-swapping," she said. "That ended long ago. Now it's called The Lifestyle." She was sitting next to me, and over the course of the evening her chair had mysteriously migrated a few inches in my direction. Every time she reached for her drink, her hand brushed my forearm.

"It's not just the name that's changed," Steve said, scratching his bicep. "The whole system is different now. The nuances are different. For example, a couple may get together and the man go with the man, the woman with the woman." He put a hand on Jim's shoulder when he said this.

I was waiting for Jim to start laughing the way he does when he's nervous, but he didn't. He patted Steve on the back like they were the best of friends, like it didn't bother him one bit where Steve was going with this.

"Or one spouse may choose to sit out and watch the other three together," Steve said. "Everything is a mutual agreement between two spouses, who choose their partners wisely, it is assumed, and together."

"Interesting," Jim said. The waiter came at just that moment, and I ordered another round of margaritas. The question that was on my mind, the question I didn't dare ask, was why they approached us on that first night, why they thought we'd be interested. Did we give off some subtle, deceptive signal that erroneously marked us as swingers?

One hour and two pitchers later, Steve looked at me and said, "Would you like to join us for a drink at our hotel?"

I was trying to figure out how to politely refuse when Jim blurted, "We'd love to."

Rebecca and Steve went out to hail a cab, leaving us alone for a moment. "What the hell are you doing?" I said.

"Lighten up," Jim said, kissing me on the cheek. "It's just a drink."

In the taxi, I took the front seat and stared ahead at the black road melting into the darkness, while the others carried on a lively conversation in the back. In the rearview mirror I could see Jim sitting between the Thompsons. Steve's hand rested on Jim's thigh, and Jim wasn't doing anything about it. Once, before we were married, Jim had said, "In the sex department, there's nothing I wouldn't try once," but I thought he was just trying to impress me.

Soon we were at the Westin Regina in a room clearly designed for romance. Suite 127 had a high white ceiling and marble floors, a king-sized bed with red sateen sheets, a heart-shaped hot tub in the corner. We were all standing around trying to act casual, and Steve was looking grateful, and my husband was looking inquisitive, and Rebecca was looking at me, and, feeling that I had to defend myself, that I had to set things straight, I said, "The last time I kissed a girl was in the fifth grade. We were playing spin-the-bottle at Marnie Topeka's house." I remembered Doris with her closed eyes, her puckered lips, the look of sheer excitement on her face as she kissed me. The kiss lasted only a second, but after that I felt I'd done my duty, and I never answered her phone calls again, never went to another one of her lonely birthday parties.

Rebecca stood by the door, her hand draped over the knob like a woman in a seventies-era advertisement. The moment we walked into the room, she had transformed into the poster girl for Miss Elegance Perfume. She walked over to me and put a hand on my shoulder. "Mary," she said. "May I call you Mary?"

"Okay."

My name isn't Mary. I don't know how she came up with it. I have to admit it made me feel a little more relaxed, though, being a Mary, as though I wouldn't have to live with the consequences of whatever happened here. Whatever happened here would be Mary's problem.

"Good." She had slipped her hand under my blouse and was tracing my spine with one finger. My skin felt very hot. "You should know, Mary, that we're not going to ask you to do anything you don't want to do. Okay? This is all about what *you* want."

Steve moved toward me, and I was wondering if psoriasis was contagious, and I was half hoping they'd pull out an Amway brochure or a Church of Latter Day Saints pamphlet, and then we could all have a good laugh because this had been a big misunderstanding, and the Thompsons would confess, a bit awkwardly, that all they ever wanted to do was sell us shampoo or eternal life.

But then, without a word, my husband began to unbutton his shirt, slowly and with purpose. He pulled it off, revealing his tanned skin. Then he sat on the end of the bed and took off his shoes, his socks. Down below, an ambulance raced by, sirens howling. Red lights slid over the walls, the dresser, the bed, the faces of those three strangers, eager and waiting.

BOULEVARD

On the day we met V., there was snow in the mountains. We were in a small town in Sweden, five days into a two-week vacation, seven months into our marriage. We were traveling through the Nordic countries by train, trying to make a baby. We hoped to have three children. It seemed like the perfect number, possessed of an innate symmetry—a beginning, middle, and end. My husband and I had both been only children, adored and lonely. Our parents were dead. We desperately wanted to have a family, to fashion from our gene pool a new and better history.

The village lay in a valley dominated by a very blue lake. Our hotel had been written up in the *Times* as one of the most romantic hotels in the world. It had a small restaurant, with a fireplace and cozy wooden tables, where one could eat fresh trout from the lake. One night after making love, we went down to the restaurant, sleepy and famished. It was a bit early for dinner, and the room was empty except for the waiter and one other patron, a thin man with an oddly shaped moustache. He was drinking coffee with whipped cream; a partially eaten piece of chocolate cake lay on the table beside his elbow. We spoke to the waiter in the few Swedish words we had learned, but our pronunciation was poor and the thin man immediately pegged us. "North Americans," he said, smiling.

My husband gave him a little nod. "Yes."

"My compatriots. How are you liking this country?"

"Very much," my husband and I said simultaneously, although neither of us had any details to back up our assessment. We both responded to the awkwardness by taking our napkins from the table and spreading them across our laps. It occurred to me that we must seem like one of those couples that have become so melded in opinion and personality as to have the substance of a single human being, rather than that of two separate individuals.

The man said, "I've been here for three years. It's a splendid country, but a bit too clean." He sipped the last of his coffee, stood, and asked, "Mind if I join you?"

There was no way to refuse him. So we spent the evening with the stranger, who told us about his childhood in Michigan, college in New York City, and his subsequent hiring by the government. "You caught me at the tail end of my first posting," he said. "Next week, I leave for Bucharest. You must visit me there."

"Definitely," my husband said. I don't know what it was about the stranger—some combination of confidence and desperation, perhaps, his utter refusal to accept any terms less than immediate friendship—but I knew that we would, indeed, visit him in Bucharest. And I knew, somehow, that our relationship would last a very long time, that there was no way of getting out of it, should we ever want to.

That night in bed, while my husband slept, I imagined our trip to Bucharest. I would wear one of those front-carry contraptions, our baby pressed snugly to my chest, as we trod the desolate streets with our new friend, seeking some fresh adventure. I would read to our baby from Romanian children's books. Years later, in college, our children would tell their friends about their adventurous upbringing, how they had been blessed with parents who traveled, how they had witnessed great political movements, nations in transition. They would talk of their eccentric Uncle V., the family friend whose relationship to their parents was never entirely clear. They would be able to tell these stories in many languages, and their faces would be the kind of faces whose nationality is not readily apparent. Our children would seem, to people upon first meeting, residents not of one particular country, but of the world at large.

But things would not be so simple. We did not make a baby in Sweden or in Bucharest the following year. We did not make a baby in Tirane, our friend V.'s third posting. On each of our trips to his far-away countries, we set to the task with renewed vigor, hoping, perhaps, that there would be something in the water, that our bodies would respond in some magical way to the change in geography. *Our* bodies, I was prone to saying. My husband allowed me to say it; this was part of his ongoing diplomacy, the cordial way in which he approached our marriage. But we both knew the pronoun was merely a defense against my singular failing: *my* body did not respond. Not to the miracle of fertility drugs, not to the thrust and rush of him, my determined husband, year after year after year.

Through no fault of V.'s own, at some point I came to associate him with the emptiness that defined our marriage. He appeared the moment we first began trying to get pregnant, and each time we saw him we were trying still. If he knew the depth of our despair, he never let on. I believe he viewed us as the ideal couple, a unit complete in ourselves, and I believe he envied our apparent romance, the false symmetry of our lives.

***

Nine years later, my husband and I find ourselves standing on Roberto Diaz Street. My husband is holding a large plant in a heavy ceramic pot. V. is attempting to hail a cab while struggling with an enormous cactus. If we weren't so tired and hungry, the vision of his small head peering from behind the massive cactus would be very amusing.

The wind upends a basket on the balcony across the street and sends a stack of newspapers flying. The papers flap down the alleyway like frantic gray birds against the backdrop of colorful houses. My husband's plant is losing leaves, and there are no cabs in site. As we wait, a tall, dark-haired woman appears from a house across the street. She glances at us, then quickly starts to walk in the opposite direction. But V. has seen her. "Elena!" he shouts, moving the cactus in a sort of wave. The wind whips his cheeks to pink and lifts his fine brown hair into a kind of spiral above his head; it is not a bad look for him. At fifty-two, he looks more like a British pop star than an American diplomat.

The woman comes over, kisses his cheek, and they exchange a few rapid words which I can't understand. The woman seems distracted, as if someone more interesting is waiting for her somewhere. V. makes introductions, translating as he goes. "Elena is my very good friend," he says. She kisses each of us in turn. Her cheek is warm, and I imagine a fire going in the brightly painted house from which she emerged. I imagine it is a house full of glass figurines, a house where lively parties are held, to which V. is not invited.

A blue cab comes roaring down the street. My husband and I share the back seat with the plants. V. takes the front. As we're pulling away, I can see Elena hurrying in the other direction on painfully high heels. A gust of wind catches the hem of her skirt and lifts it above her knees, revealing the pale backs of her thighs. V. gives a command to the driver, and then we're moving rapidly past elegant shops with elaborate doors.

"How do you know Elena?" my husband asks.

"I found her through a friend. She's a masseuse. She's amazing."

"Very pretty," I say. I know my husband agrees, though he would never admit it. He is gentle in that way. We've been married for almost ten years, and he is still able to pretend I'm the most attractive woman in any room.

"Do you hire her services often?"

"Once a month." V. turns around in his seat and winks. "No happy ending, though, if you know what I mean."

The driver slams on the brakes to avoid a man in a red coat and pants who has appeared in the middle of the road in front of us, juggling bricks. Naturally, the juggler isn't doing a very good job of it. Those can't be bricks, I'm thinking, but yes, they are. V. hands the man a coin, and the car lurches forward. I imagine that by the time we reach the next intersection, the coin will have already declined in value, its purchase power reduced from a loaf of bread to half a loaf. We arrived just as the economy is imploding; in the streets one can sense not so much panic as a kind of bracing for the storm.

From the moment we arrived, everything has happened very quickly and in a language we don't understand. Earlier today, V. met us at the airport with a hired car and took us to his spacious apartment to drop off our things. We were drained from the seventeen hour flight, both of us stunned by the unfathomable news I had delivered to my husband this morning. Still, V. refused to let us sleep. "The city looks better in daylight," he said. "We must see it now."

"While seeing the city," he added, "there is a small errand in which I will need your help, the matter of the plants. The veritable jungle in my apartment has gone to ruin during my recent travels in the interior, so I need to purchase replacements." The plants we now hold in our laps are much beloved for their medicinal properties. The needles of the cactus can be boiled to relieve stress, and the leaves of the plant my husband holds can be crushed and steeped for digestive purposes. The latter is said to bear beautiful red flowers, but it hasn't blossomed yet, and the rough, brownish leaves give off a bitter smell.

Our journey will end at the harbor at dusk, where we will meet V.'s most recent lady friend, Sylvana. I am not looking forward to meeting her. Over the years, in the various countries where V. has been posted, he has introduced us to a number of women, each of whom seems a bit less friendly than the one before.

To this day, we do not really know what V. does for a living. The words information and education are often used when his work comes up, though we've never gotten a clear idea whom he is educating, concerning what. In the time we've known him, he has held five different postings. The walls of each office are covered with plaques from various embassies thanking him for his excellent service. The size and luxury of his housing is evidence of the fact that he is in good standing with the U.S. government. Yet each posting is more obscure than the last, and somehow more desperate. He began in Stockholm and ended here, in a place that never makes the news, a capital that surely not even one American schoolchild could name, a country so small and unknown that no guidebook has been written about it.

"Why here?" we say each time we arrive at his new posting, lured by V.'s promises of great food and offbeat adventures.

"I'm looking for something I've never seen before," he says. In each new country, we end up at some rowdy party populated by North American expats half his age—artist types and acrobats, people living off trust funds or the proceeds from roadside jewelry stands. The parties always leave me feeling a bit queasy. I can't help but wonder what basic characteristic my husband and I share with the other guests.

***

We began our taxi ride this afternoon on the inland edge of the Boulevard of Heroes, a wide, straight thoroughfare that runs the width of the city from the airport to the harbor. Each major road intersecting the boulevard is named for a national figure. There are, of course, the usual suspects, noble men and women who briefly freed the people from the tyranny of various interlopers—Spaniards, Portuguese, and the much-loathed Canadians, whose dealings with this country have been uncharacteristically cruel. There are streets named after poets and philosophers, one for an opera singer of great beauty, another for a painter whose abstract and whimsically colored visions of his country, painted on enormous sheets of corrugated tin, hang in the halls of important palaces and museums throughout the world. But there are also streets named after inventors of odd things—such as the man who created the fragrance for school glue—and a street devoted to a self-declared prince who was the pretender to the throne of England. Traversing the Boulevard of Heroes, one has the feeling of traveling through a fairy tale, a proud nation's fictionalized version of itself.

"Are you doing all right with those plants?" V. asks now, in a voice that seems unnaturally cheerful.

"Lovely," I say. V. doesn't seem to hear me. He keeps looking anxiously at my husband, waiting for a response.

"Oh, we're fine back here," my husband says. But I can see that he's breaking out in a rash, splotchy red patches emerging on his neck and hands. When we first met, he was immune to everything, but over the years he has become increasingly allergic, and we never know what might set him off.

"You okay?" I whisper, catching his eye.

He nods, reaching over to squeeze my hand. On this particular afternoon, nothing can get him down. I just told him the news early this morning, as our plane flew over a vast topography of white-capped mountains, from the darkness of the Northern Hemisphere into brilliant daylight: he's going to be a father.

****

The light turns yellow just as we're approaching Anna Menendez Avenue.

"Who was Anna Menendez?" I ask.

"A martyr in the revolution," V. explains.

"Which revolution?"

"That's cause for speculation. Some say it was the People's Revolt of 1887, others claim it was the Seamstress Rebellion of 1929. It seems there was an Anna Menendez involved in both events, although it's unclear whether the two Annas were related—or perhaps even the same person. There are others who claim that Anna Menendez never existed, that it was simply the pen name of a housewife who composed, at great risk to her life, several pamphlets criticizing the government."

"A mystery," my husband says.

"Yes, it's part of the charm of this country. Day to day, in matters ranging from the price of a quart of milk to historical facts, it's impossible to unravel any definitive truth."

Just as the light switches from yellow to red, a group of schoolchildren appears and begins to cross the street in a great display of disorder, pitching forward against the wind. The children are sporting a uniform consisting of a thin white lab coat over blue jeans, with bright yellow shoes. Around the necks of their lab coats they wear a big piece of red fabric, tied in a floppy bow. Most of the children look a bit stunned, as if they were rudely awakened from their naps, but I imagine that is merely the effect of the cold. They are uncommonly beautiful children, with wide eyes, high cheekbones, and glossy hair.

It looks as though they're on some kind of Red Cross field trip, or an amusing jaunt from science class, judging by the outfits. V. explains that the national uniform was designed by the fifteen-year-old daughter of the Ministry of Education. The Minister, a widower whose interest in education stems mainly from an exaggerated devotion to his only child, made a statement on national television in which he claimed that the uniforms would not only unify the school children, but would also present a positive image abroad.

"I cannot imagine for my own daughter, or for the daughters and sons of this country, a calling higher than physician or actor," the Prime Minister is rumored to have said, although V. notes that he did not actually see the broadcast himself.

"It's entirely possible," he says, "that I heard a faulty translation."

***

Three years after our first trip to Sweden, my husband traveled there again on business. I took a few days off from the hospital where I work and accompanied him. The conference he was attending was only an hour's drive from the town where we first met V. We decided to stay in the same hotel, in the valley beside the very blue lake. It was a strange decision, but looking back, I begin to understand it. I think the deep-seated Catholicism of our childhood took hold, and we gave into superstition. We thought we had done something wrong the first time around, and that by returning to the exact place of our original failing we might make amends.

We were in the hotel for a week. We made love six nights in a row, although the terminology is perhaps inconsistent with the act. I wore new lingerie, he was extensive in his foreplay, and yet there was a feeling of labor about the whole thing. We'd both lost that old craving for one another's bodies. The thing we desired was a baby; we were no longer lovers, merely collaborators, like business partners who share the same goal. On the seventh day, after lunch, drunk on three martinis, I faked an orgasm for the very first time. He didn't even bother to fake one, he simply rolled off of me in the middle of things.

"What are you doing?" I said. "Why didn't you finish?"

"I can't."

"You have to."

He was looking at the ceiling. He'd begun to go a little gray. "It's all become so clinical."

That afternoon I sat alone in the solarium, which was flanked by high glass walls overlooking the lake. Several heaters were going, and it was uncomfortably warm. Against the back wall there was a sign that said "Health Bar." Behind the glass bar was a single basket of fruit and a vast array of hard liquors. I wore a new black one-piece I had ordered from a catalogue. It fit badly, and I felt self-conscious in it. I had read in a magazine somewhere that dieting decreases one's chance of getting pregnant, that being slightly overweight may actually increase the odds. As a result, I was plump for the first time in my life. I looked down and saw a body not my own, pale and bloated, somewhat like my mother's had become in the years before she died.

Once again, as on our first trip to Sweden, the mountains in the distance were white-capped, so picturesque as to look fake. One of the pools was half in and half out of the solarium, and there was another heated pool outside, covered with a blue tarp. Earlier in the day it had been snowing, but now it rained. Rain pelted the tarp, and steam rose up from the gaps. Mist moved across the mountains in the distance. Rain dropped from one of the indoor eaves into a small rock garden. For a while it was very quiet, and I was alone save for the bartender. Then he came out from behind the bar to turn on the jets in the hot tub, and their mechanical gurgling sound was added to the rain. I caught him glancing at my legs, and, feeling ashamed of their new heft, I covered them with my robe. I was aware of the irony—my new weight made me look somewhat maternal, asexual, like a busy mother who had let herself go.

The rain picked up. Another staff member appeared and began folding towels. A couple of minutes later another one came to light the candles around the pool. They talked among themselves and kept glancing over at me, lying mute by the pool like an overfed fish. I had the uncomfortable feeling of being at the center of a great commotion of which I was not a part.

***

"You must be my eyes and ears," V. says, turning around in his seat. "When we meet Sylvana, you must watch her body language closely and listen carefully to her intonations."

He is addressing my husband, not me. It has always been clear that V. cares for my husband more than he does for me, that his jokes are calculated to make my husband laugh, his stories designed to pique my husband's curiosity. I have been, from the beginning, little more than a prop on the stage, an inexplicable yet somehow necessary element in the slowly evolving drama of their friendship. Without my ongoing presence, I doubt they could have become friends; it would seem almost improper in a way I can't quite explain.

"What am I looking for?" my husband says, moving his plant slightly to the side. The rash is slowly creeping up his neck, but he doesn't seem to notice.

"For her intentions. I've always been inept at judging the motives of women. I don't know if Sylvana is attracted to me, or if she merely views me as a friend. Does she genuinely enjoy my company, or does she simply tolerate me because she believes I hold a position of power? I hope it's the former, because I like her very much. I'm past fifty, you know. I can't be a bachelor forever."

V. sighs. It's a terribly sad sigh, one I've become familiar with over the years. We'll be having a perfectly innocuous conversation, and suddenly V. will retreat into melancholy. My husband and I have never figured out what exactly triggers these fleeting bouts of depression. We know only that V. has some secret in his past to which he occasionally alludes. "I've known tragedy in my life," he said once, during a long, starchy dinner at an empty restaurant in Tirane, Albania. I wanted to ask him to be more specific, but then the chef came out with half a carafe of wine and a basket containing three pieces of hard bread.

"Our best," the chef said, placing the basket in front of V. with a great show of ceremony. It was just a couple of years after the revolution, and everything was hard to come by in Tirane: flour, salt, fabric, electronic goods. As the chef stood by in his impeccable white jacket and white hat, waiting for V. to give his approval, we all sat staring at the meager offering of bread, trying to hide our mutual embarrassment.

"Thank you, Leni," V. said. "It looks delicious."

The spell was broken, and in our room that night, a large suite on the sixth floor of an utterly deserted hotel, my husband and I speculated as to the nature of the tragedy. Speculation was all it amounted to, though. V. had a way of getting us to talk in great detail about our lives without ever revealing much about himself. We had known him for four years, we considered him one of our closest friends, yet in some ways his essential character was as unknown to us as a stranger at a dinner party. That night in Tirane, as a matter of course, my husband and I engaged in an unusually acrobatic bout of lovemaking. In the middle of our exertions we were interrupted by the loud jingling of a bell and the shouts of a man standing directly below our window.

"Hello, American tourists!" the man shouted several times, until finally my husband wrapped a towel around his waist and went to the window.

"What?"

"Here for you I have Albania's most glorious ice cream!"

"No, thank you."

"Yes, but later, I will be here, and you will come down for ice cream."

At two a.m., after my husband had fallen asleep, I went to the window and saw that the man was still there, waiting patiently by his cart. "You are ready for ice cream now!" he said—not a question, but a statement of fact.

I pulled on jeans and a sweater and went down to the dark street, where I bought two cups of pale yellow ice cream that was frozen so hard it was inedible. I left the ice cream on the windowsill that night, and by the morning it had thawed to a creamy slush. We had it for breakfast and were surprised to discover that it was quite good, if not very sweet. It reminded me of the ice cream that was served at Vacation Bible School when I was a child, which was always slightly tainted with the taste of the wooden spoon.

***

After a few minutes of driving in silence, V. says something to the driver. V. is a chameleon of language, able to learn a new vocabulary and accompanying set of dialects with astonishing speed. The car comes to a halt. "I wanted you to see Phelan Avenue," V. says, waving his hand to indicate a narrow, tree-lined road intersecting the Boulevard of Heroes. The trees have enormous trunks and big limbs draped with moss. They remind me of my childhood home, of summers in the American South.

"Named for?"

"Kevin Phelan, a great translator who is single-handedly responsible for saving the works of Ivan Martinez from certain obscurity."

"*The* Ivan Martinez?" my husband says. "Author of *The Dockside Trilogy*?"

"Exactly."

While I was still a sophomore in high school and my husband was studying film at UCLA, years before our paths crossed, he took a graduate seminar devoted to Martinez. The author died at 34 of an unexplained trauma to the head, leaving behind a single book. The novel was required reading for college English majors all over the country for a brief time in the eighties; now, however, *The Dockside Trilogy* has been out of fashion for several years.

"Every copy I've seen of the novel contains the line, *Translated by anonymous*," my husband says.

"Two weeks after completing the translation," V. says, "Phelan dropped dead of a heart attack. His wife never allowed Phelan's name to be associated with the manuscript. She found Martinez's work to be morally objectionable."

"On account of the sex?" I ask.

"Apparently the book had a few too many happy endings for Mrs. Phelan." V. glances around to make sure we got the joke.

"Ha," my husband says. He manages to say it without sounding insincere. This is his greatest gift—an almost ridiculous capacity for sincerity.

I do remember a particularly exuberant sex scene in *The Dockside Trilogy*, which takes place in the hold of a tiny boat tied to the docks during a hurricane. I was never able to figure out the logistics of the scene—how the couple manages to do what they do while the wind wails around them at ninety miles per hour—but I remember being impressed by Martinez's knowledge of female anatomy, his ability to make the whole thing seem both inspired and sordid at the same time. Not long ago, I read the scene aloud to my husband. The reading had the desired effect, and we spent the better part of one November weekend in bed together. The following Monday, I looked out our bedroom window at a mailbox wobbling in the wind, the driveway littered with orange leaves, and I realized that our passion was a thing unto itself, a reason to celebrate. For years we had held out the hope that it would lead to something more, something grand, nothing short of a life. But our love was worth something in and of itself, was it not? It was an accomplishment, a testament to that first spark: our love, through the years, had changed but not died. It had grown bigger, more complicated, more necessary. There comes a time when what started as a possibility, a hope, becomes both a reality and a given. An essential part of one's existence. We had long ago reached that point. I realized, then: I could live without a baby, but I could not live without him.

We pull back into traffic and continue along the Boulevard of Heroes. The light is beginning to fade. As dusk sets in the city becomes less glamorous; the night brings out its dinginess. A giant billboard towers above the boulevard. One half of the sign bears the likeness of a scantily clad woman holding a drink to her lips, advertising Salte Ron, and the other half is a white background with enormous black print: *El cambio está cerca.*

"What does that mean?" I ask.

"It's the national slogan. *Change is near.* The country is so politically and economically volatile, the slogan almost always rings true."

On the radio, some tinny local music is playing. I glance over and see that my husband's rash has spread to his face. Still, he is smiling, as if nothing could intrude upon his happiness.

***

In Danzahar, V.'s fourth posting, we simply gave up. We had not made love in almost a year. We could not separate the act from the goal, and because the goal was unreachable, the act itself became a reminder of everything we couldn't attain. For the first time, we did not embark on our vacation with the secret hope of making a baby. Maybe we were there to see V., maybe we were there to see the country. More likely, we were there to escape one another, the overwhelming solitude of our day to day lives.

If V. sensed the change in our relationship, the defeat we had both accepted, he did not show it. He was a more enthusiastic guide than ever, taking us for several days to the countryside, which seemed in its peaceful greenness to be a separate country than the one represented by the destroyed capital. On the final day of our visit he insisted on introducing us to a woman named Gavrijela, by his description an energetic blonde of indiscriminate age who worked for the railroad company. Because the railroad had been decimated by the civil war, she held the job on paper only, subsisting on a token salary and the profits she made from selling small plastic bags of laundry detergent.

V. thought it would be a wonderful idea to surprise her, and against our objections he insisted on driving to her apartment on the outskirts of the city.

"Shouldn't we tell her we're coming?" I asked.

"She doesn't have a phone. I haven't seen her in months because she's been away visiting relatives. Trust me, she'll be happy to see us."

We wound through potholed streets lined with bullet-riddled buildings. The war had been over for some time, but I could not help but feel the presence of death. The quietness of the streets, combined with the rapid way people moved—as if always looking over their shoulders, dodging an unseen bullet—lent a feeling of hopelessness to the place. V., who would normally keep up a running monologue, pointing out one landmark after another, noted a couple of ravaged government buildings and then, apparently at a loss for any viable tourist attraction, switched the subject to Gavrijela.

"She is the cleanest woman I have ever met," he said enthusiastically. "She washes her hair twice a day, using nothing but cold water and a couple of drops of baby oil. You'll see, she has exceptional hair. And she's very intelligent; she taught herself English." He was quiet for a minute. "Don't tell her I told you, but she might be the one. If things work out, I might even stay in Danzahar indefinitely."

Evening was falling as we approached Gavrijela's part of town. There were no lights on in any of the buildings. "They haven't had electricity in this section of the city since the war," V. explained.

We stopped in front of a five-story rectangular building that looked more like a barracks than an apartment house. The building was made of blackened brick, with only a few small windows to interrupt the monotony of the façade. There was a hole in the front of the building where the door should be, and the entrance was littered with leaves and trash that had blown in from the street. V. took a lighter from his pocket, and we followed the tiny flame up a concrete staircase to the fourth floor, then made our way down a hallway so dark it might have been midnight instead of six o'clock in the evening.

"This is it," V. said, stopping in front of a door at the end of the hall. In the flickering light of the flame his face looked so childish and eager I could not help but feel a kind of maternal affection. We had never given him anything, yet he had always opened his door to us, had always introduced his romantic interests to us with the unflappable optimism and barely disguised nervousness of a teenage boy introducing his parents to his first girlfriend. Always, it seemed, he was looking for our approval.

The door opened slowly. A young woman stood in front of us, holding a long, tapered candle. "Hello," she said, almost as if she were expecting us. "Come in."

V. let his lighter die. Gavrijela closed the door behind us. The darkness felt absolute; I groped for my husband's hand.

"I'll light more candles," Gavrijela said. She didn't seem at all perturbed by this intrusion of strangers into her home. She went into another room and came back with several candles. She placed each candle in its holder, forming a semicircle around the room, lighting them one by one. As the room grew brighter, Gavrijela's features became clearer. Her blonde hair was pulled back from her face in a ponytail, and her chin receded slightly. Her eyes were very blue, her teeth exaggeratedly small. I realized she could not be more than twenty-three.

I do not know who noticed it first. My husband was occupied with a stack of books in the corner, but V. and I were both watching Gavrijela, the careful way she lit the candles, as if it were some elaborate ritual. She was standing in profile when I noticed the snug fit of her T-shirt, the way her belly protruded from her thin frame. Just then, while she was lighting the final candle with one hand, she brought the other hand to rest beneath her stomach, cupping it gently.

I glanced over at V. He was staring at Gavrijela, open-mouthed, truly shaken for the first time since I had known him. My first impulse was envy—that, and even anger. Anger that he could have accomplished such a feat, this man who had always had such poor luck with women, this man who moved from place to place, never staying long enough to settle. My husband and I had been trying for so many years, doing everything we were supposed to do, monogamous and determined and, ultimately, unsuccessful.

V. took a couple of steps backward and sat heavily in a chair, momentarily unable to muster the stream of phrases that had always carried him effortlessly through every social situation. My husband, oblivious to the whole thing, picked up a copy of an English-language novel and began asking Gavrijela questions about the book. As they chatted about the writer, whom Gavrijela had studied at the university, V. took a deep breath, closed his eyes, and leaned his head against the chair. He only stayed that way for a few moments, Gavrijela didn't even notice, but I understood then that he had never slept with her. Perhaps she had never had any romantic interest in him at all.

By the time we left her place, V. had completely regained his composure.

"She's nice," my husband said. He has never been one to notice details, and I realized that, absorbed as he had been with the conversation about the American author, he had no idea that Gavrijela was pregnant. "Who knows. Maybe next time we see you, you'll be married."

"I've had a change of heart," V. said, looking forward into the darkness as he expertly steered the car over the black, pitted streets. "She's a bit young for me."

Several months later, we received a postcard from a tiny country we'd never heard of, bearing his usual neatly printed message: *You must join me here for good food and offbeat adventures.* Of course we came. We could not help ourselves, although if you asked us to define the nature of our attraction to V., the exact terms of our affection, we would be unable to formulate an answer. We simply go to him, year after year, country after country, as if something mysterious in his nature, or ours, demands that we do so.

***

The Dockside Trilogy opens with a poem. Martinez was by no means a poet, and the poem is not very good. The faulty meter and awkward line breaks, combined with the poem's political subject—an unidentified revolution in an unidentified third-world country—make for tiresome reading indeed. Most of the critical papers on Martinez simply gloss over the poem, as if it did not even exist. It is a gruesomely bloody poem, in which a difficult birth is used as an extended metaphor for the revolution. The gist of it is that, after an arduous labor, touch-and-go for nineteen hours, the baby lives, but it is shriveled and bluish, and it will clearly be a very long time before the baby can survive outside of an incubator. At the end of the poem, the mother is *hanging on to life by a thread*—Phelan's translation actually employs that phrase—and as a reader you have no idea whether or not she'll make it. It's a cheap ending for a squalid little poem, and in his anonymous "note from the translator," Phelan writes, "I was tempted to do more than translate. I was tempted to simply edit the poem out of the text altogether. But a desire to be true to Martinez's intention prevented me from doing so, unfortunately. If the baby were omitted, *The Dockside Trilogy* would cease to be a tragedy, and might arguably be called a comedy instead."

***

The driver rolls the window down, and I can smell the fishy odor of the harbor in the distance, mixed with diesel fumes. My legs are sore from the pressure of the large pot resting on my lap. I shift the plant so as to see out the window more clearly. The car slows to a crawl.

"Is traffic always this bad?" my husband asks.

"There was an election two weeks ago," V. says. "They've been having parades almost every day, but the festivities are usually over by early afternoon." He glances at his watch. "We're supposed to meet Sylvana in five minutes."

Moments later, the car comes to a complete halt. Traffic in front of us isn't moving at all. Up ahead, at the intersection, a long procession of cars and brightly decorated horses makes its way down the avenue.

"The Avenue of the President," V. says. "The city's most celebrated avenue. Presidents change so often here, it makes more sense to name the avenue after the office itself rather than a specific president."

The driver, who until now has been completely silent, opens his car door, steps into the street, looks skyward, and lets out a celebratory yell. Then he climbs back in the car and shuts the door as if nothing had happened. He turns around and says something to us, gesticulating with both hands.

"What's he saying?" my husband asks.

"He says change is coming. He says change is good. He says this new president will turn the economy around, and this is a bright new day for his country."

"What's your opinion on the matter?"

"Every president promises change, but each administration is almost identical."

Again, pain shoots through my legs. Up ahead, the harbor lights are shining. Car horns are honking, and a troupe of trumpet players passes on the parade route.

"Sylvana must already be there," V. says. "The restaurant is within walking distance of her work, and she's always precisely on time." He sounds nervous, as if something monumental depends upon this meeting. The wind has settled down, and a fine rain begins to fall. "We'll have to eat inside," he adds, more to himself than to us. Already, his plan for the perfect evening is beginning to fall apart. I imagine Sylvana gathering up her purse and running inside. Checking her watch, perhaps, ordering a drink without us.

A girl of about sixteen approaches the car. She's wearing a short black skirt, high heels, and a T-shirt that bears the new president-elect's likeness. Her hair and face are damp from the rain, and she's carrying a cardboard box filled with small bottles of Salte Ron, the national drink of choice. She holds the box up to the window. She must have pegged us for Americans, because she says in a quiet and precise voice, "Please to buy?"

V. pays no attention to the girl, lost as he is in his thoughts of Sylvana. But the driver reaches into his pocket and drops a large silver coin into the girl's hand. The girl accepts the coin, hands him a bottle, and moves on. The driver does not open the bottle, but instead places it aside and sits with his hands on the wheel, looking ahead. "A souvenir!" he says, which makes me wonder how much English he is able to understand. Has he been listening to us all along? In the side mirror I can see his face, calm and happy.

The parade route is a flurry of sound and motion, but the traffic on the Boulevard of Heroes is halted. It feels as if the world is moving rapidly in some positive direction, while inside the car we sit utterly still, transfixed and waiting.

I look over at my husband. The rash has spread all the way to his elbows, tiny welts have begun to appear on his neck, but he doesn't seem to notice. He is staring out the window, more relaxed than I've ever seen him, ecstatic in his belief in the coming family.

In the front seat, V. takes a small mirror out of his messenger bag. He holds the mirror low, as if to hide his vanity from us, and pats down his hair. He opens his mouth and smiles, turning his face from side to side to check the cleanliness of his teeth. Then he quickly slips the mirror back into his bag.

Down at the harbor, Sylvana is waiting. What has V. told her about us? And does she really care for him, or is she merely another one of his fantasies? For a moment, I feel the secret pang of the selfish parent. I am ashamed to realize that I do not want Sylvana to be the one for V. I do not want her to love him. I do not want her to upset this delicate balance. Isn't V., after all, in part a product of my husband and me, of our odd and lengthy friendship? And aren't the three of us, in some way I have never before allowed myself to admit, perfect for each other?

V. has become impatient. "Let's walk," he says. He presses a large stack of cash into the driver's hand and opens his door, beckoning us to follow. My husband steps into the street, cradling the large plant in his arms. As the driver begins to count the cash, the traffic in front of us creeps forward. My purse strap catches on the broken seatbelt and I struggle to release it. The car lurches forward. V. notices my dilemma and reaches in, swiftly releasing my purse, taking my hand, and helping me out of the car. On the street, a small crowd begins to form. A shirtless man opens a bottle of Salte Ron and pours it over his head in celebration, showering me with the warm liquid. V. does not let go of my hand. We move quickly, our threesome, on our way to meet V.'s new love. A woman comes toward us, long dark hair, blue dress, arresting green eyes, and for a moment I think it must be Sylvana, but she keeps walking, the rough fabric of her dress brushing my arm as we pass. This city is filled with beautiful women. We pass them, one after the other. I gaze into the excited faces, certain that I will know her when I see her—the one who has captivated our beloved V., the one who may, at last, steal him from us.

"Cambio esta cerca!" someone shouts. He pumps his fist in the air, tentatively at first, and then again with authority. Another voice joins in. And another. The chant rises up from the crowd, just a few voices at first, and then hundreds: "Cambio esta cerca! Cambio esta cerca! Cambio esta bueno!" The crowd of dozens quickly becomes a crowd of a hundred, a thousand, even more. I've lost sight of the restaurant, I've lost sight of my husband, I've lost sight of V., and yet I can still feel his firm, sweaty hand pulling me through the masses. Sylvana is nowhere, or perhaps everywhere. The noise is intoxicating, deafening, I can't think, I can't see. There is a sense of joy, of celebration, but also, unmistakably, of fear. The crowd has grown so large and fast that it is impossible to know where this will end. The bodies converge around me, a sweaty mess of elbows and knees, heads and hands, signs and banners. An older woman slides her arm around my back and pulls me toward her, as if to dance. Something crashes on the ground, blocking my path. The plant my husband had been holding lies on its side, the pot broken. I bend and reach for it, but V.'s small hand pulls me forward. Salte Ron rains down from the sky. Change is near.

ACKNOWLEDGMENTS

I wish to thank the editors of the following magazines, in which these stories previously appeared, sometimes under different titles: "Hum" in *The Missouri Review*; "Medicine" in *Playboy*; "Lake" in the *Mississippi Review*; "Scales" in *Logorrhea: Good Words Make Good Stories*, edited by John Klima, and *Best American Fantasy 2007*, edited by Jeff VanderMeer and Ann VanderMeer; "Hospitality" in *Mid-American Review*; and "Travel" in *Stories from the Blue Moon Café II*, edited by Sonny Brewer. Special thanks to Linda Swanson-Davies and Susan Burmeister-Brown at *Glimmer Train* for providing a wonderful home for several of my stories over the years, including "Hero" and "Boulevard."

Thanks to my amazing agent, Valerie Borchardt, for more than ten years of friendship and support. Thanks to Allen Wier and The Fellowship of Southern Writers. I'm grateful to Dan

Waterman at the University of Alabama Press, the incomparable Rikki Ducornet, and the folks at FC2 for making this book possible.

As always, thanks to Kevin, for the honeymoon and everything else.